FROM BOYS
TO GENTLEMEN

From Boys to Gentlemen

Chris Daughtery

Copyright © 2014 by Chris Daughtery.

Library of Congress Control Number:		2014915348
ISBN:	Hardcover	978-1-4990-6646-3
	Softcover	978-1-4990-6647-0
	eBook	978-1-4990-6645-6

All rights reserved. No part of this book may be reproduced or transmitted in any form or by any means, electronic or mechanical, including photocopying, recording, or by any information storage and retrieval system, without permission in writing from the copyright owner.

This is a work of fiction. Names, characters, places and incidents either are the product of the author's imagination or are used fictitiously, and any resemblance to any actual persons, living or dead, events, or locales is entirely coincidental.

Any people depicted in stock imagery provided by Thinkstock are models, and such images are being used for illustrative purposes only. Certain stock imagery © Thinkstock.

This book was printed in the United States of America.

Rev. date: 08/26/2014

To order additional copies of this book, contact:
Xlibris LLC
1-888-795-4274
www.Xlibris.com
Orders@Xlibris.com

Contents

Chapter 1	Boys Will Be Boys	11
Chapter 2	Who's Ya Daddy?	21
Chapter 3	Fathers, Where Art Thou?	30
Chapter 4	I'm Grown	37
Chapter 5	When It Rains, It Pours	42
Chapter 6	Interventions	48
Chapter 7	Re-breaking Bones	59
Chapter 8	Everything That Glitters Ain't Gold	71
Chapter 9	Where Did You Learn That?	79
Chapter 10	What if She Meant Something to You?	92
Chapter 11	We Are Overcomers by Our Testimonies	105
Chapter 12	Misery Loves Company	116
Chapter 13	Blessing or Curse? Only Time Will Tell	125

This book was inspired by so many people. God is *number* one! And I don't say that to sound cute. I truly mean that what he has put in me and shown me in my life has inspired me to write this book.

Next come my grandfather, grandmother, wife, and sons. My grandfather introduced me to God, and my grandmother was the strong hand of correction and redirection in my life. My wife pushes me closer to him, and my sons hold me accountable, knowing that the way I live will speak louder than my words.

Last but not least, everyone that has had a part in my life, especially my kids at the recreation centers and detention centers. Whether you told me your life story, spit in my face, kicked a door in, allowed me to pray with you in your cell, got restrained by me, told me that I'm the closest thing you ever had to a father, hit someone with a plunger, told me why you are in a gang, told me why you hate church, or told me why you do the things you do, you uncovered my eyes to an issue that I was ignoring. You have truly changed my life. So thank ya'll.

This world is full of males—human beings that are born with the Y chromosome as part of their DNA, people that are a little more physically developed on average in comparison to the average female. The supposed providers, protectors, breadwinners, husbands, sons, and fathers of this world.

Notice that I used the word *supposed* for all the titles I just named. These are things that we were ordained to do by the Lord. Our job is to work the earth and provide for our families. We were called to be the head of the household. We were taught to love our wives as Christ loved the church. We were charged to train up our children in the way they should go; and when they are older, they will not depart. We were called to teach our sons to be men.

The problem is that you have to be much more than a male to be and do the things I speak of. You have to be a man. I'm going to make a valiant effort to save a near-extinct breed of male—someone that not only possesses the male reproductive organ or the physical stature, but has also been trained to be so much more.

Join me in the cause to create more gentlemen.

Chapter 1

Boys Will Be Boys

When a boy is brought into this world, there is such joy. Everybody wants to hold him and tell the mother how cute he is. Unless it's an ugly baby, then everyone just says "bless his heart." It is all fun and giggles for a week or two. Then you come off cloud nine and realize that this baby is not a toy or a trophy but an amazingly complicated responsibility. Whether you see the child as a blessing or an accident, it is too late because he is here. So the parents are forced with the life-changing decision of either stepping up to the plate and raising this amazing creation or passing the child off to other hands. It's sad that it is now an option for children to leave their children with their parents. All the comedians make jokes about how Big Mama is gone, how Grandma is twenty-six and Great-Grandma is thirty-eight. The funny thing is that this isn't funny; it's true. Babies are raising babies. A boy can only teach a child to be a boy. I'm sure you have heard the saying "Boys will be boys."

In a small West Texas town called Eneliba, there was a young girl named Tomika Carter. She was full of life and dreams and all the light in the world to give. She had the world at her fingertips, and there seemed to be nothing present on this earth capable of slowing her down. She breezed through school and climbed to the top of her class with hard work and God-given smarts, not to mention an unwavering desire to be the best in everything she did. This girl didn't care if the task was sharpening her pencil. She wanted the sharpest pencil in the class.

Tomika never knew her father and had a very impersonal relationship with her mother. Her mother was always there and provided for her but never really showed her daughter any type of affection. Tomika would bring home award after award, and her mom would always give her the same weak smile as she told her, "Good job, honey," lacking any type of enthusiasm or interest.

Her mother's lack of emotion had two effects on Tomika. The first was a positive effect on her. It fueled Tomika's drive to impress her mother and to gain the desired reaction. She never stopped trying to win her mother's approval. The second effect was not so positive. Even though she worked toward obtaining the appreciation of her mother, each time she didn't accomplish her goal it fed an inner issue of never feeling good enough. 6

Tomika strongly inquired about her father as a young girl. Tomika's mother continued to avoid any question asked by her daughter. When the young child became too persistent, she would lash out at her, shouting, "Why do you want to know about that man? Am I not enough for you?" Overwhelmed with guilt, Tomika would surrender her search for the knowledge of her father. The poor child ignored her desire to know about this for quite some time.

But one day, Tomika was in class when she was informed by her teacher that the school was having a daddy-daughter day. It was simply an event where the fathers spent the entire day with their little princesses. At the end of the evening, there would be a ball for the young girls to dance the night away with the man that they loved most in the world. At this moment, Tomika made up in her mind that she was going to find out where her father was. The entire way home on the bus was a dry run rehearsal on how she was going to navigate through the usual responses of her mother. She came home and walked into the kitchen with a mission. She sat her bag on the kitchen table and walked to her mother as she was washing the dishes.

She took a deep breath and said, "Now, Mom, I know I'm not supposed to ask about him, but there is a daddy-daughter day tomorrow and I wanted to know if you would help me call Daddy so he could come and I could get to know him. Wait, Mommy, before you say anything, I'm not trying to say that you aren't enough. I love you, but I just want to meet my daddy, Mom. All the other girls' daddies are going to be there. Please, Mommy. Please."

Tomika's mom began to shed tears that had been built up for years. She could no longer hold back the truth. She turned to her daughter with a look of despair in her eyes and whispered, "Baby, your daddy left. He doesn't love you, and he doesn't want you. When you were born, I called him and told him that he had a baby girl. He told me that he didn't have no dang baby girl. He didn't want you, baby. I don't talk about him 'cause he left us. I spent six years trying to get him to come and see you. Every time you asked about him, I swallowed my pride and I called him. But every time, it was the same broken promise. He swore he would come, and I wouldn't hear from him for months. I can't call him anymore, baby. I just can't do it. He doesn't love you, baby."

Tomika's eyes filled with tears. "No, Mom. All daddies love their baby girls. I don't believe you! It's not true!" The young child ran to her room and cried herself to sleep, continuously whispering, "Why didn't he want me? Why doesn't he love me?"

From that moment on, Tomika did all she could to hide from the hideous truth. She found her escape in school and sports. Tomika was truly making a name for herself in sports. She had lettered in four sports as a freshman. Now it was normally against the tradition of the school to put freshmen on varsity. But imagine being the dummy that has Lebron James on the JV team. She was a natural-born athletic specimen. She loved many sports, but her true love was basketball. The coaches would even go as far to say that Tomika was the best basketball player in the state of Texas, period. The boys didn't like that, but none were willing to attempt to prove the statement false at the risk of personal embarrassment.

After breaking every individual record in the book, she was interviewed for Athlete of the Decade at her high school. Tomika was asked what her biggest dream and greatest fear were. Her eyes opened as wide as could be, and she proclaimed with great confidence that she was going to take whatever college she attended to four consecutive national championships and was going to be the first woman in the NBA. She laid out her plan to graduate in three years so she could have her senior year to work on graduate school and her proposal to enter the NBA draft. She also explained her business plan to be a multibillionaire by the age of thirty. The interviewer was lost in a daze from how bright the young lady shined. This child so free, determined, and able appeared invincible. The reporter would shortly see just how wrong her assumption was.

Tomika was then asked to disclose her deepest fear. Her face transformed from this energizing glow to an agonizing pit of sorrow. It was as if a rose in full bloom wilted to its death right before her very eyes. Tomika's lips began to quiver, and her eyes filled with tears as she gave a blank gaze into the distance. She was unable to hold back the pain that flooded to its opportunity to escape from its previous place of submission. With a demoralized whisper, she uttered, "My greatest fear is that I will never know why my daddy didn't want me, and that he will never love me." The interviewer immediately stopped the camera and wrapped Tomika in her arms. Tomika simply repeated "Why doesn't he want me? Why doesn't he want me?" as the tears streamed down her face.

Up until this point, everyone thought that Tomika was carefree. She had become a master of keeping people at a distance. Even in her personal relationships, she was always able to deflect any attention aimed at her on to others. She never allowed herself the time to think about any of her issues. She rarely had a second that wasn't consumed by sports or schoolwork. She always appeared to be happy and in good spirits. Yet this simple question brought this untouchable juggernaut to the most vulnerable of states.

Tomika continued on to bring a third state championship to her high school as well as being number three in a class of eight hundred. She had earned a full ride to almost every college in the country but hadn't decided where to go. On graduation night, Tomika went out to celebrate. She was coaxed into going to a graduation dance with her teammates. "Look, Tomika, there is nothing for you to study for. There is no game film for you to watch. You already skipped our prom, so don't try to get out of this. It may be our last night together."

The young girls begged for thirty minutes straight. She finally gave in. "Okay, I will go. But if I don't like, it I'm leaving," she stated with great authority.

The girls arrived to the dance, and as Tomika walked in, all eyes were on her. Oh, wait, I didn't tell you, did I? Tomika was BAD! Hold on. Let me translate for those of you that aren't following me. Tomika was absolutely beautiful. She had long black hair that appeared to be a waterfall of black silk flowing from her head, the deepest dark-brown eyes, butter-smooth skin, with a smile that could retire the sun. Yeah, I know that last one was corny, but if you saw her smile, you would see how fitting the description really is. She was by far the most-desired girl in the entire school, and for the first time in her life, she actually felt like it. This was the first time she had ever paid attention to the effect she had on guys as she walked by.

She had always desired attention from guys. The problem was that no guy had a chance with her during school because she was so focused on class and basketball. This was a new ball game,though. School was over, so there were no academics or sporting events to stand as a barricade. She was fair game and let the best boy win. The boys at the party had allowed their hormones to overwhelm them. It was as if all of them had reverted back to sperm racing to the egg but only one of them would obtain the prize. She danced with guy after guy and received the worst of the worst pick-up lines that brought her nothing but great laughter. She still seemed to be unobtainable. But as usual there was one out of the many that caught her eye, Julian Ward.

He was smooth, charming, handsome, and said all the right things. He didn't harass her like the others. He simply walked up to her and asked her to dance as if she was the only one present in the room. After drawing her away from all the other drooling buffoons that lacked his swagger, he took her to the dance floor for a slow dance that he had organized with the DJ. Julian made her feel like she was Cinderella at the ball. He ended a magical dance with the softest of kisses, and at that moment, Tomika was engulfed with a flurry of emotions she had never felt. Her naïve young mind asked, *Is this what love is?* For her this was just like the movies.

Sadly that was the only reference to love she had ever known. What the entertainment industry had taught her was as real as it came. Julian asked her if she wanted to leave, and she vigorously nodded her head with no hesitation, not leaving any chance for the invitation to be retracted.

They drove out to a spot at the lake where the moon and the stars reflected off the water. They had a long talk. Julian seemed to be interested in learning everything about Tomika. He asked her everything, from her favorite color to what she planned to be doing when she is sixty. This made her comfortable with him and gave her a sense of trust. For the only time other than the interview she expressed her pain of the lost love of her father.

"Okay, Tomika, let's play secrets. I'm going to tell you three things that I never told anyone, and then you tell me three. Okay?" Tomika laughed and agreed. "Okay, secret number one. When I was fifteen and I stayed in New York for a summer, I took ballet." Tomika erupted in laughter! Julian quickly tried to explain. "There was this pretty girl up there and she smiled at me. The next thing I knew, I was in some tights, jumping around on my tippy toes."

Tomika continued to laugh as she asked, "Well, did you get the girl?"

Julian shook his head. "She said that I was cute, but she liked football players, not dancers. It was embarrassing, but at least they let me keep the tights. Okay, secret number two. You remember junior year when a guy streaked at homecoming game? That was me."

Tomika was shocked. "Dang, boy, you should have run track. I ain't never seen nobody run that fast."

"That is because I was so scared. Once the cops came on the field, all I could think about is what if they take my mask off and my mama finds out?"

This was too much for Tomika. She had never laughed this hard in her life. The mood changed a little bit for Julian's last secret. He looked up at the stars as if he was searching for something. "Well, secret number three is that at times, I wish my mom would leave my dad. He cheats on her, and when he gets drunk, he hits her. He always talks his way out of it. He blames her for making him so mad, and she goes right along with it. It makes me so mad. But I can't be that mad 'cause it works on me to. I feel like such a coward."

Tomika did not like the way the statement made her feel, so she quickly changed the atmosphere with her own secrets. "Okay, it's my turn. Secret number one. Brace yourself 'cause this is nasty. One time at a tournament, this girl fouled me hard and I almost hurt my knee. So after we beat them, we went to go eat at the mall and we saw her and her team. She was talking to this guy and she had on this skirt. I happened to be on my period, so I did the unthinkable. I went to the bathroom and took out my tampon, and while she was talking, I put it at her feet. Then I walked up and interrupted their conversation and told the guy that I think she dropped something. She was so mad she couldn't even defend herself. She just started screaming and crying."

It was Julian's turn to laugh uncontrollably. "Are you serious? Now that is nasty, but, man, that is funny. I wish I could have saw her face."

"Okay, secret number two. I have always had a crush on Mr. Caldwell."

Julian was dumbfounded. "Are you talking about old-as-dirt, smells-like-mothballs, false-teeth Mr. Caldwell?"

Tomika responded shyly, "Yes. He is just so sweet. I don't know what it is. He always made me smile. And when he talked about his wife, it would just give me hope that love really does exist."

Julian could relate. "I hear you. He is a really cool dude."

Now was the moment of truth. At this point, she was waging an inner war with herself. *Should I tell him my one true secret? I feel like I can. I want to, but what if I start crying?* Julian placed his hand on her shoulder and told her, "I know there is something that you wanna say that has been a burden on you. I just want you to know that I know what that feels like. It is hard to explain, but I trust you. You can trust me too. Tell me, Tomika, so you don't have to suffer alone."

This was the encouragement that she needed to open up. "Secret number three is that I never knew my father. I do my best to never let others know, but I have felt so worthless and ugly since the day my mama told me that he never wanted me. So I view other men the same way. If my own daddy didn't even want me, then why would someone else dare to want me?"

Julian turned to her and stared in her tear-filled eyes and said, "Tomika, I have liked you for so long. I used to come to all your games and meets. I never knew that you felt this way 'cause you always seemed so happy. I thought about talking to you a lot, but I watched the way you shut all the others guys down. I feel like I know you so well. I want to tell you something, but I don't know if I should."

At this point, Tomika's interest was fully captured by what the young man was holding back. "Don't do that to me, Julian. Tell me please. You said it yourself that you can trust me."

With perfect timing, Julian grasped Tomika's cheeks with his hand, firmly yet so gracefully. He softly brushed her hair away from her face and looked into her eyes as if he was searching for her soul. He took a deep breath and he said, "For so long, I have wanted to tell you that. . ."

This five-second pause seemed like a five-hour pause. Tomika attempted to encourage him to continue. "Don't be afraid just say it, Julian."

He composed himself from the dramatic pause and said, "Tomika, I love you." For the first time, she heard the words that she longed to hear from a male. Instantly she felt free. Her deceitful heart ignorantly accepted this false claim with glee. For her the search was over. In her fragile little world, she was loved. Tomika didn't know quite how to show her appreciation for the gift that Julian had given her. Julian saw no need to hear Tomika say it back. He asked her, "Tomika, will you make love to me?"

She felt that this is what comes next. At first she was hesitant. There was such a new flurry of emotion and physical sensation surging through her at that moment. As he grasped her and began to kiss her, she stopped him for a second and asked him, "Are you sure you want to do this? You could probably have any girl you want. Why me?"

He simply replied, "I don't love those other girls. This is what people do when they love each other." The last bit of defense that Tomika had was shattered by the confirmation of his proclaimed love for her. She gave herself to him with no further resistance, and she felt loved.

She went home that night with pure joy. She had no idea what she had done. For this brief period, ignorance was bliss. She could not believe how lucky she was. She had found her true love. She was caught between shouting everything from the rooftops or waiting to call her girls and tell them about her step into womanhood. The next day, she was still floating from what she thought was her glorious night. She called her teammates to tell them the news, but she was too late. Julian wasted no time spreading the word of his newest victim. For Julian, Tomika's virginity was nothing more than extra props from his boys for being the first to hit it. It didn't take long for word to get back to Tomika. She could only say to others and herself, "But he said he loved me. He looked me in my eyes and told me he loved me." She murmured to herself as she paced back and forth outside his house, waiting for Julian to return. "Surely, this is just a misunderstanding. People get stuff twisted up all the time."

After a few hours of waiting, he finally came back with his father and several friends from playing basketball. Julian was shocked by her presence and attempted to not acknowledge her. Tomika's voice cracked as she mustered out, "Julian." He turned to the troubled soul that had called his name with sweaty palms and a racing heartbeat. Tomika could not speak clearly. She had to know, but she didn't want it to be true. She stood there for a second with not a word spoken by either of them. *This awkward silence must be broken*, she thought. Her eyes were filled with tears. It felt like she had a lump in her throat the size of a grape fruit, but she proceeded on asking, "Julian, did you . . . did you do what they said . . . was it real?"

"Was what real," he replied, attempting to appear oblivious to her request.

"Last night. What we did and what you said to me."

Julian stood there like a deer caught in headlights. At this moment he realized what he had done. He wanted to live up to the hype that his boys and father held him to, but he truly didn't want to cause the girl any further pain. So what was he to do? Attempt to provide relief to the Tomika's ravaged heart by telling her how he really felt, or continue the charade that kept his peers and father calling him the man? In the heat of the situation, he thought that he was just saying what needed to be said to get what he was looking for. He looked at her then back to his friends and father and said, "Naw, it just sounded nice at the moment."

This arrogant and hateful response gained much approval from his peers and father but caused catastrophic damage to a blameless young girl. He faked a smile, put his hand on her shoulder, and said, "Hey, we had a good time, so just leave it at that." He turned away and walked into the house, leaving the poor girl shattered. He had never felt so low, but he was quickly brought back up. His boys gave him dap and admired his player ways. His father put the dagger in Tomika's heart as she heard him say with pride, "That's my boy! I didn't think you'd been listenin' to me about these lil hoes. You handled that like a true playa. I thought she had you tripped up there for a second, but I see you get ya game from ya daddy."

Tomika stood there paralyzed by the pain. She stood on that sidewalk for almost one hour, staring at the door, until her teammates came to get her.

It seemed as if Tomika would never recover from that day. She ran into the house to tell her mother what had happened. "Oh, Mama, this hurts. He told me he loved me, Mama. He said that he loved me. We made love, Mama. Why, Mama? Why would he do that?"

Her mother methodically took another drag of her cigarette and turned to look at her distraught daughter. She said to her with no care, "Well, Tomika, boys will be boys. That's just how they are. They will say whatever they need to say to get what they want. Don't worry about it. Ya daddy told me the same thing. He may be the first, but he won't be the last. You just have to deal with it. Go ahead and wash up for dinner."

That statement rang in her head: "Boys will be boys." Tomika was hell-bent on proving this statement to be untrue.

Tomika left for college that next August. Instead of focusing on her dream of the NBA and business plans, she spent two years trying to find herself in man after man. She was determined to recover that piece of her that she had lost that night with Julian. Those were two of the darkest years of her life. She fell for any man that said he loved her. She lost herself in an expedition for love only to find a treasure of men's lust. Her physical beauty compounded this problem. The men she attracted knew nothing of her as the beautiful queen she was. All that was seen was a pretty face and the curve in the rear of her jeans. Her ignorance of what love was rotated her in a cycle of sexual exploitation. In attempt to cope with the pain, she lied to herself. She supplemented love for sex. So she told herself that every guy that wanted to sleep with her loved her.

This would show to compound the issues that were already present. In one case, she had gone to a party with a guy she was seeing. After some drinks, he took her to one of the rooms, and they began to have sex. A few seconds later, three more guys came in. Shortly after, two more came. They all took their turn with her. She asked for them to stop, but they didn't listen, and she was too intoxicated to fight. When she told the second guy to stop, he told her, "Shut up, hoe. You know you want it." The part that hurt her the most was that physically, it was pleasing to her. She enjoyed the sex even though she didn't want it. This confused her into believing that what happened to her was her fault because it felt good.

After two years, she was given a blessing that was confused as a curse. She went to the hospital for what she thought was the flu to find out she was six weeks pregnant. She was devastated because she had no idea who the father was. *Was it Mark, or was it Mike? Or maybe it was Shawn.* She continued to feel lowered by the second as she realized for the first time just how many men had used her. She made up her mind at that moment that love was not real. No more searching for this phantom emotion that brings nothing but pain. She became bitter. Every man that she saw was guilty of the abuse she suffered. *Mama was right. Boys will be boys.*

She was so enraged that she prayed to God for the first time in her life. It was her last resort. She looked to the sky and said, "I hear that you are up there and you help people. So I have one request of you. Oh, God, please allow me to have a daughter so I won't have to hate my son."

Her first voluntary conversation with the Lord was to spare her the pain of dealing with another man. This request was not answered because it wasn't God's will. After her son was born, she added another man to the list of those who abused her. She truly felt God hated her, so she put up walls around her heart that allowed her to become the coldest of the cold.

On a faithful spring morning, a bouncing baby boy was born to Tomika. She named her son Julian to remind her to never try to love another man.

Too many people are judged off the surface of their circumstance. On first look, Tomika would have simply been labeled as a slut or a hoe. I'm sure plenty of people are ready at this very moment to proclaim how they have been through so much more, how they didn't to turn to this, and how her behavior cannot be excused. So for those people, let me stop right now and give you a hand clap for being born psychologically stable enough to make the right choices of action for these types of circumstances with no type of upbringing or training. Please know this statement is saturated with concentrated sarcasm. It is that attitude that has this world in the condition it is in now. God has called us to not just be saved but to spread the gospel. It should hurt your heart as a child of God that this girl could go through this with not one person bringing her to the Lord. The Word says to train up a child in the way it should go and when he is older he will not depart. So answer this for me. If an air force general took you to an air force base and told you that you have three hours to fix the engine on the F-22 Raptor, what would be your response?

The number one response would be "I don't know anything about this machine, so how can you ask me to fix it? No one has trained me or given me any direction." You would more than likely get unanimous understanding from the world about your situation. It's just not right for you to be asked to do something that you haven't been trained to do. It takes years of training and school for this type of job.

So now my question is why we can't find that same compassion for a child that was never taught to be a gentleman. That same understanding for a young girl that was never taught what to look for in a man and hasn't ever seen a true example of what a man is. You can only teach someone what you know. Whether it is right or wrong, it can be taught. Our babies are being left to fend for themselves and learn from whoever they can, and we have the nerve to complain and condemn them for how they come out?

Chapter 2

Who's Ya Daddy?

How did you learn to be the way you are? Who taught you to play basketball? Who told you that you were beautiful? How did you know to open the door for other people? Who taught you to tie your shoe? Who did you want to be like as a child? The saying goes that anybody can be a daddy, but it takes a man to be a father. But for my personal preference, the term *daddy* holds more connection and intimacy.

When a man is attempting to drag his baby boy's first word out, he doesn't make himself look like a complete fool telling the child, "Come on, say 'FAAAA THHH ERRR'" The term they long to hear is *daddy*! When a young girl wants to ask for something, she will rarely say, "Oh, Father, can I please have some new shoes?" She is going to say, "Daaadddddyyy, you know I love you, right?" I'm sorry for hating on your game, young ladies, but you know that it is true.

The daddy is possibly the most distinguished position in life. You are given the honor of being in charge of the lives of a family. This is a job so essential to the life we fight for each day. The problem is, when a father doesn't do his job, that doesn't mean the job is no longer present. It simply means that someone or something will be put in his place.

Tomika's son was here. Whether he was planned, wanted, or needed was irrelevant. A child was here and had to be cared for. Tomika did an amazing job to make sure that her child was provided for, yet she failed to raise him. She gave him hardly any love or nurturing. Does this sound familiar? Often we allow history to repeat itself. Julian James Carter continued to grow nonetheless. He had a very rough time with not knowing who his father was. This lack of information made him very reluctant to reach out to people. It seemed that everyone around him was going camping with their father or having some type of father-son outing. Julian hardly ever spent a day where he didn't wonder where and who his father was. But his mother made it ever so clear that this was a forbidden subject.

He did what most people do. He found something to help him cope with the pain that he didn't have an answer for. Julian placed these unexplained emotions into basketball. The young boy was in a world to himself, hardly noticed by the rest of the people he shared time and space with each day. By the time he had reached the seventh grade, he was a sight to behold. Puberty had gone full drive for him. He had the build of a grown man. He was a pure athlete and as bright as the North Star. Julian hated his name for reasons he couldn't seem to explain, so he went by JC.

School was all a game to JC. Sports were all he cared about. His physical talents were immediately noticed by the coaches of his school. JC had crossed over into a new era of his life. Things were different now. Before he was pretty much flying under the radar. He never really got involved with any teams or clubs. He was a shy and soft-spoken boy that just accepted the status quo for what it was. This was no longer the case for young JC. He was exposed to a whole new environment in where he would have to find a way to adapt. And adapt is exactly what he did.

Upon the first day of practice, JC was doing what came natural to him. Sadly, that was destroying anyone that had the courage or ignorance to attempt to guard him. He had amazing ball control, a simply sweet jumper, and the ability to jump out of the gym at will. His coach stood in awe as JC blazed down the court and appeared to explode from the ground with a determination to administer unnecessary abuse to the rim. The five-foot-eleven-inch, 190-pound teenager was as rare as they come. The coach hadn't even seen college ball players with skills he presently possessed. On that day, JC would never be the same. People began to flock to him, attempting to reserve their place on his bandwagon. Word spread like wildfire about the middle schooler who was dunking like he was in the NBA. Girls threw themselves at him while guys seemed to have auditions to be his new best friend.

At that moment JC was transformed from a shy young boy to an arrogant know-it-all overnight. He began to take full advantage of the people that seemed to throw themselves at his feet. Tomika became concerned that JC had began to sell drugs because of all the clothes and electronics he was receiving.

When he came home that day, Tomika called him into the living room as she flipped through a magazine to avoid eye contact. "Julian, we need to talk. I need to know where you getting all this stuff from."

JC took a deep sigh and said, "Mom, you know I hate it when you call me Julian. I got it from some girls at my school."

Tomika's eyes rose from reading the magazine and locked on her son. "What do you mean you got it from some girls? What did you do to get it? Why are they buying you things, and who are these lil girls?"

JC stood there baffled by the emotion his mom began to show. "They just bought it for me. I didn't even ask for it. If they gonna buy me stuff, I'm not gonna turn it down."

In an unexpected burst of rage, she jumped up and grabbed JC by his shirt as she cried and screamed, "You are going to take this all back to them and tell them you are sorry for what you did to them. I won't let you do to them what they did to me! I won't let you, Julian! I will kill you before I let you do it to them!"

"Mom, stop it! What are you talking about? I didn't do anything! Stop, Mom!" he shouted.

His mother continued to shake him and yell for a brief moment, then she caught herself. She wasn't yelling at her son; she was yelling at Julian Ward. After realizing what she had done, she commanded JC to go to his room. JC was so lost. He couldn't gather what his mother was trying to tell him. He left the house to seek his refuge in the only way he knew. His sanctuary was the court. Nothing else mattered when he was able to play. He was free from this world he didn't understand.

While he was out playing, Tomika attempted to calm herself. Even she didn't understand what had just happen to her. At that moment, all she could see was herself standing on the sidewalk that day. She was fighting an internal war. Everything in her wanted to love her baby. But she was held captive by the fear of falling victim to another man, even if it was her own son.

The next day JC went to his game and did what he knew to do. He had twenty-seven points, thirteen steals, fourteen blocks, and nine rebounds in the first half. It was like Dwight Howard decided to go play pick-up at a local boys and girls club. The opposing team forfeited to save their children from any further embarrassment. The secret was out. JC was a beast. Forget high school. Colleges found themselves scouting a thirteen-year-old.

JC was not prepared for this curse that seemed to be a blessing. Mark Davis, JC's coach, could not help but see this goldmine he had stumbled upon. He knew that he had to get a hold of the boy before anyone else did. He brought him in the office after the game. He said, "Son, you are amazing. My phone has not stopped ringing since the game was over. Come over here and have a seat."

JC sat down, and Coach Davis put his hand on JC's shoulder. "This world is full of bloodsuckers that only care about themselves. They will tell you whatever you want to hear and promise you the world. But when you can't give them what they want, they will be gone as fast as they came. Now let's be honest. You could possibly be the best player I have ever seen. This will open doors for you that others only dream about. Now from what I have heard, you are a pretty smart guy. But if the schoolwork ever becomes too much of a distraction from your game, you let me know. I got a lot of pull with the superintendent. I scratch his back, and he scratches mine.

"Now let's talk about the top two things your talents will bring you. The first one is money. I can look at you now and tell that people are gonna do everything they can to get on your bandwagon. They won't even see your face. They will see dollar signs. The second thing it will bring is women. Are you a virgin, son?"

JC paused for a second. The truth was that he had not even had a real conversation with a girl. But as socially retarded as he was, even he knew that it wasn't smiled on to be a virgin athlete. It was like an unspoken badge of manhood to have sex in his eyes. Before JC had the chance to lie, the coached continued, "I'll take that as a yes. But don't worry, son. Soon you will have any girl you want and as many as you want. They will flock to you. Now, with that, there is one thing you must learn now. Don't get tied down to these lil girls trying to get a free ride. They will either try to get pregnant by you or trick you into thinking that they love you. They just see money. Trust me, son. You are too young for love. You can find love later. Right now, just enjoy getting all you can get. Are you listening, son?"

JC just nodded his head. He had never had a man take interest in him like this. He had found his first taste of a father. "Now remember, if anyone comes asking you questions about anything, you tell them no comment and to come talk to me. Hey, son, I know that I haven't known you that long, but I knew that you were special the first time that I met you. I love you, son, and I'm not going to let anyone hurt my boy. I'm here for you."

JC smiled big and said, "I got you, coach. I love you too." He was so blind to the intentions of the coach. He was just happy that he thought someone loved him. JC took every word his coach said as gold. He had found one person in his life that loved him. Even after he went to high school, JC kept in close touch with his coach.

Over the next couple of years, he wasted no time taking advantage of all the perks he could receive. He talked to girls as if they were cars he was planning to test drive. He really began to get into rap. Several rap stars became his idol. Every album, mix tape, video, or concert ticket that was available was in JC's possession. Everything from his clothes and hairstyles to his mindset about money, cars, and women was based off the young music superstars. JC had become a boy that parents warned their daughters about. It didn't help that JC's actions were widely accepted by his peers. Unlike his mother, JC frequently went to a church youth group. You would think that this was a good thing. But this only gave JC a misrepresented view of what Christianity was. The leaders of the church were too lost in the number of people that came to the youth meetings because of JC to give him any correction. They feared that if he was offended, then people would stop coming. So the pastor turned a blind eye to JC. No one was getting saved, especially not JC. The youth group became the number one source of JC's sexual partners. To make it worse, many of the leaders encouraged and participated in JC's activities. The one leader that spoke out about what JC was being allowed to do in the church was alienated, asked to leave.

JC was doing what other guys only saw on TV. He was having his way with girl after girl with no problems, until he ran into Cherish. She was not so willing to submit to JC's ways. Her rejecting him only made him desire her more. He began to pursue her with great effort. He attempted to be what he called romantic by giving her an expensive pair of shoes and bag that he got from some other girl her size. But Cherish was not into all that.

One day, JC was talking to some of his teammates in the locker room about the young lady. "Bro, I don't know what's going on. I ain't never had to work to get a girl. They just come to me. And the ones I go too pretty much rape me. I don't get it. She got me trippin'."

One of the boys wasted no time giving him foolproof advice. He stood up with an evil smirk and told him, "Bro, if you want to get in that, all you have to do is drop those three lil words."

JC was completely captivated by the boy's newfound information. "Well, what are they?" JC inquired.

"All you have to do is tell her that you love her and she will give it up, bro. My pops taught me that. It works every time. You just look at her, take a deep breath, and say, 'Girl, I love you.' Then you step back and watch the draws melt off of her like butta."

JC replied with a confused look, "But I don't love her."

The rest of the guys busted out in laughter from his response. "She don't know that," the boy explained.

JC didn't feel right about the advice. A girl's emotions were never involved in his previous encounters. They knew from the start that this was just sex and maybe a little hangout time if you were fine. Another one of his less-popular teammates spoke out and said, "Man, that ain't right. A female is not just a toy to be played with. She is a queen. You shouldn't lie to her just to sleep with her."

He was quickly interrupted and mocked by the rest of the guys. "Wait a minute, ain't you a virgin? You wouldn't know what to do with a girl if you could get one. Come on, JC, are you gonna listen to this guy? You knock down more girls in a week than he ever will in his life. I know you ain't gonna go out like that."

The young man grabbed his bag and walked out, completely embarrassed by his teammate's comments. What the young man had said made JC think, but that thought was almost instantly wiped away by the louder voice of his other teammates. It was clear that he had one desire in mind. So JC talked himself into trying it.

He ran up to Cherish after school and pleaded with her to accompany him on a date. "Come on, Cherish, just go to the movies with me. Give me a chance." Cherish had a strong interest in JC but refused to be just another name on his wall of women he had conquered. She was not won over by what most girls desired him for. The superstar athlete and bad boy role was not at all what she was about. She saw flashes of a sweet, smart, and intelligent guy. Now it didn't hurt at all that she thought he was extremely handsome. She thought for a second and saw no harm in going to a movie.

Cherish was the first girl JC had ever asked on a date. Every girl before her was simply sexual adventures to explore. This mixed with his persistence in courting her finally produced fruit. "Okay, JC, I will meet you there at seven."

JC smiled and ran off to practice. After practice, JC went home and began to think of what he was doing. This was a new level for him. Cherish was going to be the first female he had really had a conversation with. He was nervous because there was a new element to this interaction. He actually cared what she thought. Sex was his primary reason for pursuing the young lady, but that goal had taken a backseat to wondering what he was going to say to her. The mighty player had met his match. He began to practice in the mirror on how he was going to greet her. "What's good, Ma? No, that won't work. Hey, sexy. No. I see ya, lil mama. Eehhhhhh!"

JC became frustrated with his failed attempts to be smooth. This girl had him trippin. JC attempted to make himself snap out of the trance he was in. "Come, JC, what is wrong with you? You givin' this chick stuff. Daydreaming about her in class. Thinking about how good her hair smells. How pretty her smile is. How pretty she sings. Man, her hair smells good. Aaahhhhhhh! JC, snap out of it!" he began to say to himself.

This boy needed help. Due to his reputation and lifestyle, the only female that JC had in his life other than his sex partners was his mother. As he was getting dressed for his date, his mom asked him what he was doing. JC paused and asked her, "Mom, when do you tell a girl you love her?"

Tomika's heart stopped at the end of his phrase. She simply froze up and walked away. She closed her bedroom door and cried silent tears, reliving all the pain that simple phrase had brought her. JC cracked the door and watched her as she cried. He didn't know what to do, so he left her alone.

He met Cherish at the movies right next to the ticket booth. It was the moment of truth. He walked up to the ticket booth, attempting to have swag. As he approached her, he tripped and almost fell on his face. Now we can add embarrassment to the new array of emotions that he had come into. Cherish laughed as JC performed a gymnast-like move to keep from busting his face on the cement. JC just stood there frozen, watching as everyone chuckled. Cherish walked over to him and asked through her laughter, "Are you all right? I couldn't tell if you tripped or you were break dancing."

Now, as humiliated as JC was, he could not help but render a smile and sniggle at the young girl's witty comment. "Oh, you got jokes, huh," he replied.

All through the movie, JC found himself simply staring at Cherish. Any time she would look at him, he would quickly look back at the screen to prevent getting caught staring at the young lady. After the movie, they walked to the car. "I'm not ready to go home. Do you want to go to get something to eat?" he asked.

Cherish placed her hand on her chest and said with great sarcasm, "Dinner AND a movie. Oh my, how did I get so lucky?" They both laughed as they entered the car.

They grabbed some burgers and went to the park. JC could not help but notice that he was becoming quite fond of Cherish. He had never really taken the time to actually communicate with the opposite sex. He had actually forgotten his primary intentions for the date and was simply enjoying her company. They laughed and talked for hours. "This is really nice," JC said to himself.

The two of them began to spend a lot of time together. JC found himself more and more drawn to this young lady. He even began to trust her. She was the only person he ever shared his feelings about his father with. He even shared how much he longed to be closer to his mom. While they were chilling after a game, Cherish asked, "JC, why don't your mom ever come to your games?" JC fought hard to keep back the tears. Cherish did not pressure him. "If you don't want to talk about it, then it's okay."

This only made him want to talk even more. JC's guard was officially down for Cherish. "I wish I knew why my mom don't come. Some people wish for cars, money, or mansions, but I just wish my mom would hold me sometimes. I wish she would say something to me other than take out the trash or clean your room. She has always bought me whatever I wanted, but I would give it all back just to have some quality time with her. I don't know anything about her. She treats me like her liability instead of her son." JC began to lose the fight he was having with his tears as they streamed down his face. "Sometimes I really feel like I should just take my life so I won't be a burden to her. One thing that hurts the most is that I know she loves basketball. That is one thing we share. But I'm sitting on two state championships and she has never even told me that she is proud of me. I just want something with her. Something other than the questions and money. I just want something real."

Cherish held information that only Jesus knew. She had begun her own downpour of tears as she listened to him. She wrapped her arms around JC and simply held him as she stroked his head. This was something that he had never experienced but was one of the most precious moments in his life. She had surpassed anything that JC had ever had before. She was his friend, and he truly cared about her. Their constant appearances together demanded attention at school. Initially they thought Cherish had become yet another name in JC's track record. But that rumor was quickly squashed. People took fast notice to the care that JC showed. This was different.

Now Cherish was not the date-around type. She was a virgin and was waiting on that special guy to sweep her off her feet. Her dad was a single parent and worked a lot but did everything he could to make sure his baby girl had what she needed. He always told her to find a man that loves her and let him take care of her. Now everything was going fine with young JC and Cherish until one night, as they were at a friend's house watching a movie, Cherish said the wrong thing. She began to ponder on what her dad had told her and wanted to see if JC was the type of guy her daddy was telling her about. "So, JC, what are you going to do for me, and how are you gonna treat me if we make this just me and you?"

JC instantly heard the words of Coach Davis. "Don't get tied down with these lil girls tryin' to get a free ride." *She almost got me. She just trying to use me*, JC said to himself. A motiveless and innocent question snatched away all feelings he had developed. He then remembered what his initial goal was with Cherish. He played off her question and used it to his advantage. "I just want to be with you. I have wanted to be with you for a long time, and I don't know if I should tell you this . . ."

Cherish was fully intrigued and had to know. "Well, go ahead. Tell me," she replied.

This was it; he was going to test it. He took a deep breath, made eye contact, and said, "Cherish, I love you."

She was mesmerized. Cherish began to cry and hugged JC as she whispered, "I love you too." This was just what she thought her daddy was talking about. She then gave him a kiss that invited him to partake of the prize he sought after. Along with her innocence, she gave him her heart. He stopped and said to himself, *It worked, it really worked.*

It's sad, isn't it? JC has become his mother's greatest fear. So who is to blame? Well, some will say that all the blame falls on JC. No one put a gun to his head and made him do it. He is just a little hooligan, and he will get what is coming to him. Some would blame the young man that put him up to it. Others will blame his mother for not talking to him when he asked the question about love. Finally, some will blame the coach for the seed he planted. He was supposed to be a role model and leader, but he simply steered him down a path that brought him to see women as objects to obtain.

Well, you are all right. Everyone is to blame. But we are forgetting another suspect guilty in this crime. Us! Where are the examples for young men like JC to follow? Like I said in the beginning, the absence of a father doesn't mean there's an absence of the responsibility. Instead of stepping up and reaching out to these young men, we are just ready to speak of their treachery and point out the flawed decisions they make. I never knew my biological father. He left my mother and then my mother left me because she felt I would have a better life with my grandparents. I thank you for that, Mama. I didn't have my father. Yet the Lord saw fit to bless me with Papa. This man taught me almost everything I know. He didn't have to do what he did, but he chose to raise a son that didn't share a drop of his blood.

When I was older, before he got sick and died, I asked him, "Daddy, why did you take me in? I wasn't your responsibility, and you could have sent me back with my mama. Why did you keep me?"

He looked up at me with a smile and said, "You didn't have to be my responsibility for me to do the right thing. You didn't do anything wrong, so why should you suffer? I got to raise a boy I love. I feel sorry for your father, whoever he is, 'cause he missed out on you. Plus, it's what Jesus would do."

I love that man, and every day that goes by, I am teaching someone else what my daddy taught me. Thanks, Papa.

Chapter 3

Fathers, Where Art Thou?

Who is the first person you look for when you get in trouble or feel you are in danger? When a kid is upset and is ready to be avenged, the first thing that comes out his mouth is "I'm gonna tell my daddy on you." This is because the daddy is expected to protect his family. In the Word it says that before you take a house, you must first bind the strong man—a.k.a. the head of the house, a.k.a. Daddy. There are few connections made in life that are more complex and meaningful than a father and his child's. But the question must be asked: what happens when Daddy is not there to save you?

Crazy as it may sound, JC was truly hurt by Cherish. In his eyes, he had let his guard down for one second, and he was taken advantage of by this deceitful girl. *I guarantee this won't happen again*, JC said to himself. He had made up his mind that no female would get the chance to do this to him again. JC put special attention in slandering Cherish's name. He wanted her to feel the same pain that she had caused him. JC was so mistaken. While JC was ripping apart any trace of self-respect Cherish had, she was speaking of the new love that she had found. It was so real to her. She even told her daddy that she had fallen in love with this young man. "Oh, Daddy, it was just like you said it should be. He loves me and he is going to take care of me just like you said a man is supposed to do."

Her father was uneasy about this proclamation his baby girl was making about this young boy. Cherish had never talked about anyone like this before. All he could tell her was to be careful. After the weekend had passed, Cherish walked through the halls and was bombarded by the whispering and filthy looks she received. As she was walking, she spotted

JC and ran to him to bid him a good morning. "Hey, baby, how are you doing today?" she said with a smile and girlish charm.

JC looked at her and, with a hateful tone, exploded, "I ain't yo dang baby. I just wanted some, and it wasn't even that good. My coach was right. You hoes are all alike."

Cherish shifted gears quickly and sternly asked, "What the hell did you just call me?"

JC showed no hesitance in his response. "Yeah, you heard me. I called you a hoe. You let me hit it, right? We ain't together. That sounds like a hoe to me."

Cherish was unable to stand there anymore. She ran off in tears, seeming to leave pieces of her shattered heart crashing against the floor. The hallway was silent. No one was prepared for such a dramatic sequence of events. After all the fireworks, one of JC's teammates broke the ice and timidly asked, "So what was all that about, bro?"

JC boldly replied, "She tried to get me. She thought she was slick. All these hoes are the same. I ain't got time for these games. I'm 'bout to focus on making this money." The young man received no clarification from the response but was afraid to ask any other questions. There was no dap or admiration given for JC's action toward Cherish, but he couldn't have cared less. JC was all about himself now. He allowed this single incident to send him down a path that neither he nor anyone else was prepared for.

Cherish had not stopped crying since JC had verbally thrashed her. The tears continued to flow. She couldn't just drop it. She had to know what happened. She waited outside the gym for JC to come out. He came out with several of his teammates. Cherish was almost scared to call for him in front of the other boys, but she could not just stand there. So she closed her eyes and shouted, "JC, can I speak with you please?"

The rest of the guys saw who had made this desperate request and wanted no part of round two from this morning. So they continued to walk and murmur among each other. JC walked over to the young girl and rudely said, "What?"

Cherish pleaded her case. "JC, why would you do that to me? We made love. I gave myself to you. You said you love me, and I love you. You are supposed to protect me and care for me. Didn't last night mean anything to you?"

JC quickly replied, "No!"

Cherish snapped back. "So why did you tell me you loved me?"

JC stopped and thought for a second then stated, "It sounded nice at the moment. Look, just be happy that I even let you have sex with me.

So when I'm rich and famous, you can tell all your friends that you slept with me."

Cherish just began to scream and cry. This only made JC's anger flare as he yelled, "Don't even try to fool me with them tears. You tried to run game on me, and I got you first. You faked all that BS with me just so you could find out what I was gonna do for you."

At that moment she stopped crying, and all her pain became anger. "What the hell are you talking about? I meant every freaking thing I said to you! Everybody warned me that you were just trying to use me, but I stood up for you! It was all real to me, JC! Everything was real! I told you I loved you, and I mean it. But if that's what you think about me, you can burn in hell, JC, 'cause I see now that no one will ever love you! No one! Now I see why your mom is distant. You're a monster, JC. A cold-blooded monster."

JC didn't understand. Was she really sincere about all that had happened?

Cherish ran all the way home, wanting her daddy. She burst through the door and jumped in his arms and began to let her heart pour out to him. As she told her father the story, he did nothing but hold her tight and cry. "I'm so sorry, baby. Daddy is so sorry," he continued to whisper.

JC drove home and called Coach Davis for some advice. "Coach, hey, this is JC. I really need some advice. You see, I took this girl out on a date and—"

Coach Davis interrupted JC, saying, "You really got the nerve to call me, you little ungrateful bastard? After all I did, you still left me high and dry. I know that you are talking with the scout from North Carolina. I'm not going to get a dime for you going there. I told you to go to Wake Forest. Don't call me with your freakin' problems. I'm not your daddy. I don't have time for your petty complaints."

JC was speechless. He had talked to the scout from North Carolina, but he told him that he was going to Wake Forest. He never even got the chance to tell his coach his side. He was heartbroken by the one man that had ever been anything like a father to him. JC rarely ever cried before, but at this moment, he was unable to stop. It was almost as if sixteen years of built-up tears were released in that single day. As the tears flowed, all the heartbroken young child could say was "But he said he loved me." JC's sorrow was quickly transformed to rage. He had become numb to the world he lived in.

That night, he went out to some parties. JC didn't have a taste for drinking but quickly adopted the habit. He would drink until he didn't care anymore and then began his search for the next female to defile. Any girl that had the self-respect to tell him no was immediately given the tongue thrashing of a lifetime. He would verbally degrade women as if they were not human. He would tell girls that they were not worthy for him to even urinate on, let alone, good enough for him to be with. This wild and reckless behavior made JC plenty of enemies.

Later that month, JC had a big press conference to announce his commitment to North Carolina. All the major sports news and local news channels were there to get the scoop on where the young basketball phenomenon was going to lace his shoes next. JC showed up to the press conference drunk as a skunk. His loud and belligerent antics were broadcasted to the world. He stumbled across the stage and fell against the podium. After burping loudly into the mic, he boldly said, "How are all you bloodsuckers doing today? I know that all of ya'll can't wait to ride my jock and tell me how great I am, but you can skip all that. Just send me some hoes to the locker room so I can celebrate. Ha ha. No, but for real—ya'll don't give a crap about me, and I don't give a crap about ya'll. So let's not waste each other's time here. So go to hell and buy my shoes when they come out. And oh yeah, don't do drugs 'cause beer is legal, and they can't take you to jail for that."

Everyone was left speechless as JC's coaches rushed him to their office to keep him away from the chaotic uproar that was stirring in their midst. No one could believe what had happened. People were outraged at the events that had taken place. North Carolina immediately yanked his scholarship and claimed they wanted nothing to do with a young man that would show such a lack of character and respect. JC showed no remorse for his action as one of his coaches told him his repercussions. "I'm the best basketball player to ever come out of high school. I made a commitment to a D1 college my sophomore year. Do you really think I'm gonna have a problem getting another college to jump on my bandwagon?" JC arrogantly stated.

He walked out the office and to the gym where he could play his pain into submission. JC was a complete mess, but he still held on faithfully to his true love. After the press conference, JC was about as welcomed as a black man in Hitler's army. No one wanted anything to do with him, except for Cherish. She walked in the gym and sat silently as JC dribbled his worries away. As he played Cherish saw the young man that she had first met in the park that night. She walked on the court and placed her hand on his shoulder as he was shooting a free throw and inquired, "JC, why are you doing this to yourself?"

He stopped in mid shot and slowly turned his head to her. "I'm not doing anything to myself. I'm just doing me. All these people always screaming my name and how they know me and love me, but no one even told me happy birthday today. They all fake. They just trying to use me. So why not be real and just get paid for it? All these hoes don't want to do nothing but use me, so I use them first. I'm not gonna let no chick come between me and my paper. That's what I love and that's what loves me. That's what I can count on. You was right, Cherish, ain't nobody gonna love me. Nobody."

Cherish's eyes filled with tears. Her heart was overwhelmed with guilt for the statement she had made out of anger. But just as she made the attempt to speak, the media busted through the gym doors with cameras, microphones, and questions galore. Cherish's words were lost in the noise, but all she wanted to tell JC was "But I love you, JC. I promise you I do." All she could do was watch him transform back into the frigid-hearted monster that he had become to adapt with what he had to face.

JC simply turned away with a smirk and ignored every question he was asked while he simultaneously put on a showcase of his basketball skills for the world to see. Tomika watched her son on the news and was furious! She sat on the couch smoking, waiting for her son to enter the door.

Finally that night he stumbled in. It was pitch-black, and all that could be seen was the little circle of fire that was given by the lit cigarette hanging from Tomika's lips. Through all that had happened to JC, Tomika was working two jobs to keep her mind occupied from her own problems. Needless to say, she had not paid any attention to her son's struggles. All she knew was that he had a place to sleep, a car, food on the table, and clothes on his back. It was if she never even knew that her son was going to play college ball. JC attempted to ignore the ghostlike figure on the couch, but as he walked by, his mother called to him in a raspy and pain-filled voice, "Julian James Carter, get yo tail in here now!"

He walked in and stood in front of her with his hands in his pockets and his head tilted to the side. "What, Mother?" he stated with attitude.

"Boy, who the hell you think you talking to? Have you lost your mind? 'Cause I'm so ready to help you find it. Now why were you acting a dang fool today in front of all those people? My phone has not stopped ringing all day."

JC just stood there staring off into space.

"ANSWER ME, DANGIT!"

He looked at her and said with a smirk, "I was just having a little fun."

Tomika was fed up with the disrespect that he was showing. "You better watch your tongue, little boy, and stop sassing me," she warned. "Now why did you get up there and say all that stuff?" The disturbed child gave no response. "Little boy, if you don't answer me, I'm gonna beat yo head in. I'm your mother. You better start acting like it."

His head shot up as he forcefully responded, "Oh, now you want to be my mother. I have been going through hell, and you ain't been there for nothing. All these people trying to use me and lie to me, so I told them just how I felt. Plus it sounded nice at the moment."

At that very moment, Tomika lost it. Once she heard that phrase, all the pain that had been festering in her heart erupted into pure rage. She lunged at JC and began to slap and shake him by his shirt. She had lost herself in the pain she had tried to keep in all these years. JC could do nothing but cover himself up as Tomika delivered blow after blow.

A neighbor heard the disturbance and ran over to check on them. She came in the door calling for Tomika. As she walked in, she saw her still attacking JC. She ran over to pull the near-exhausted mother off her child. Tomika finally let go of him as he laid on the floor in the fetal position. "Tomika, stop it. You have to stop," the neighbor pleaded.

JC got up bloody and bruised and stumbled to his room. "Get out! Get out now! I will be dead in my grave before I let another man hurt me! Get the hell out of my house!"

JC wasted no time grabbing some clothes and his basketball. He walked to the door and turned back to his mom and said, "I'm gone. I don't need you. I couldn't even have you if I did need you. I'm done paying for every other man's mistakes. You can't even see past them to come to your own son's game. Don't worry, Mom, you don't ever have to worry about me hurting you." He started out the door and stopped one last time. He turned back, looked his mother in the eyes, and said, "Oh yeah, thanks for telling me happy birthday."

After he closed the door, his mother continued to bleed a river of tears from her eyes.

Now I know there are so many people out there ready to point the finger now. How could JC do these heinous things? He is such a terrible person. He acts like he doesn't have any home training. Oh wait. He doesn't have any home training—'cause no one trained him. Tomika is so messed up that she is beating her son because he said something that another man said that broke her heart. Oh, we need to judge her too, huh?

But before we crucify her, let's ask some people this. I'm gonna talk to the mothers real quick. How many times have you gotten mad at your child and all you could see was his good-for-nothing daddy? I never knew my biological grandfather, but I can't tell you how many times my grandmother told me I was just like him when I did something she didn't like. Now I know we are focusing on the men—but, ladies, you have to step up for this one. Stop seeing the man instead of your child. How long must the son pay for his father's mistakes?

Now we have a young man that is truly out on his own. It is him against the world. All he knows is basketball and money. Those are the only things he can trust. What should he do? Now let me say again the things that JC is going through; and his past explains why he does what he does, but it doesn't excuse it. For instance, if a mother kills a man to protect the life of her child, is that wrong? Yes, it is wrong because we are not supposed to kill. But it is understood why the mother would take such an action. So none of JC's actions are excused, but it would be so unjust not to let them be explained and understood.

Chapter 4

I'm Grown

Oh, how wonderful it is to be grown. No curfew, no chores, no one to answer to. You are your own boss. No one can tell you what to do. Why? Because you're grown. Wrong! I don't care if you were present to help Noah pick out the wood he was going to use to build the ark. You will always have someone to answer to. Being grown doesn't just bring freedom; it demands responsibility, whether we accept it or reject it.

JC got into his car and just sat there. He finally drove out to a court to escape reality. He laid on the court and looked up in the sky and began to wonder. He had heard people talk about God before, but he didn't know anything other than that. To him Jesus was nothing more than he-say, she-say gossip and a way to get people to give their money in church. Sadly even in his time at the youth church group, he had never read the Bible and never prayed. He looked at the stars and closed his eyes, saying, "Sir, I don't know you, but if you are as real as people say, will you show me? It's so hard to believe you are real in this world. Did I do something wrong? Do you hate me? Do you just not like me? Sir, I'm coming to you because I have no one else to turn to. Please help me, sir. If you are up there."

JC had prayed his first prayer. He had no idea that he had made the first step in gaining the most precious thing a human can obtain, a personal relationship with God. As he was playing ball, a couple of local gang members recognized JC from a party. A young lady had approached JC a few months ago and said, "You look like you can make it rain, daddy." He then smiled and poured beer all over the girl and told her that was the only way he was going to make it rain for her.

That young lady just happened to be the sister of Jamal Paul. My granny always told me to be careful with people with two first names. Jamal was a member of the Vipers, the most notorious gang in all of West Texas. Jamal had been wanting to dig his fangs into JC for a long time, but his boss, Cobra, was making too much money off JC's games. Jamal was not the first person to have unfinished business with JC, but Cobra wasted no time putting the word out that anyone that touched JC would answer to him. Jamal watched as JC performed a symphony on the court as if the ball was his violin and the court was his sheet of music.

Jamal knew better than to cross his boss but quickly spread the word of JC's presence in the neighborhood. Jamal called Cobra to share the info. Cobra immediately commanded Jamal to bring JC to him. Jamal walked on the court with his boys, clapping their hands together and circling JC. "Well, well, well. To what do I owe this wonderful surprise? Julian Carter in the flesh. I am a big fan. Can I have your autograph?" Jamal teasingly stated.

JC looked up and said, "Sure can, but that will be twenty-five dollars. But judging by your clothes, you can't spare that, so this one is on me."

Jamal snapped back quickly, saying, "Well, judging by your face, you play a lot better than you fight, so why don't you watch your mouth before I finished the job your mom started?"

Julian looked up with a shocked look on his face.

"Oh yeah, I know all about the little mishap you had at home. We got people in your neighborhood. We got someone that wants to meet with you."

"And what if I don't want to meet him?" JC stated boldly.

Jamal looked back with a smirk and said, "Trust me, superstar, this ain't an invitation that you want to ignore."

After that statement, JC knew exactly who Jamal was talking about. Cobra had been to more of his games than anybody. "All right, homie, let's go," JC said, attempting to sound tough.

They took him to a big brown house that seemed to tower over the entire hood. They walked past the party that was going on in the front of the house. It seemed that all eyes were on JC as he was lead to the back. The room was filled with smoke and alcohol. It looked just like the movies, only instead of a desk, Cobra was sitting at a domino table. Cobra never looked away from his dominoes as he said, "What's up, young blood? I saw you on the news today. Now that was some funny stuff. Well, enough of that. Let's cut past the BS. Let me know what you need."

"I don't need nothing. I'm a grown man, I can take care of myself," JC exclaimed with his chest out and chin up, attempting to look as hard as possible.

"Oh, really? 'Cause word on the street is that ya mama whooped dat tail and threw you out." JC was stunned by the response given by Cobra. Cobra continued on, saying, "Look, I'm gonna give you a house up the block and one of my whips. I'm gonna send a couple of lovely ladies down there to take care of all your little boo boos too."

JC was lost. "Why are you doing all that? What you want from me?" JC asked.

"I'm just tired of people trying to run game on you, young blood. That stuff ya momma did wasn't right. You remind me of myself, so I'm gonna give you what no one gave me. You fam now, young blood. And always remember, fam takes care of fam."

"Yes, sir," JC answered as he tried to put together the puzzle that was just dropped on him. He stopped and asked himself, *Did God do this?*

Jamal and his crew took him to his new home. Jamal gave him the key and said enjoy. JC stepped into the fully-furnished house. "Now this is what I'm talking about. This is just my style right here." He took his own personal tour of the house. It was stacked with flat screens in every room, computers, game systems, pool table, and satellite. Not to mention a stocked fridge and pantry. Jamal was not happy at all but would wake up and apologize if he had even dreamed of speaking out less on taking any type of action against Cobra. Jamal and his crew left, and shortly after, the ladies that Cobra had promised came. They dressed his wounds as they undressed themselves. JC was so happy and naïve that he actually looked up to the sky and thanked God for this curse he had blindly walked into.

Tomika was a wreck. She had not left the very spot that she was in when JC walked out the door. She had cried her eyes dry. She had put her baby out on the street, and she couldn't even tell herself why. As she lay there, she heard a voice speak to her, telling her that there was no reason to live. She began to hear it more clearly. She lay there unable to move. She wanted to take her life, but she lacked the physical strength to act on it. So she kept still until she fell asleep.

The next day, JC woke up to three beautiful young ladies that had pleased him the whole night through. He got up and took a shower and had breakfast. Out of all the things that had happen the previous day, all JC could think about was Cobra telling him he was family. That word just brought such excitement to him. He had never had anyone tell him he was family. Even coaches calling him son didn't bring the same joy he received from being part of a family. He walked around the house, exploring his new home.

He received a text on his phone from Cobra. "Hey, young blood, I got a few representatives from a couple D1 colleges that want to holla at you. Get dressed and meet me at Red Lobster at two p.m."

JC was convinced that Cobra was looking out for him just like he said. He got dressed and drove to the restaurant. He walked in and saw Cobra in the corner with three men. They were recruiters from Texas, Texas A&M, and Texas Tech Universities. They spent a couple of hours just talking and laughing. Cobra was the first to get to business. "Now look, all this is nice, but I want to know which one of your schools is going to take care of my boy the best."

Texas showed no hesitation shooting down the other schools, promising playing time as a freshman, the biggest spotlight to make it to the league, and the most promising campus for his lifestyle. The other schools just couldn't compare. Cobra looked at the other two gentlemen and quickly informed them that they were dismissed. The UT rep had shattered any hopes of either of the schools landing a chance at the young superstar.

"Now that they are gone, let's get down to business. Clearly, you don't do well with press conferences. So we have to rebuild your image. You will read a public apology to the school and the world. You don't have to mean it, just read it. That way we can get you some endorsements. Maybe get those shoes that you told everybody to go to hell and buy. Hey, I got an idea. We will make you the victim. We will tell everyone you were just stressed with what happened between you and your mom."

JC quickly stopped him. "You leave her out of this. I have no mother!"

The rep immediately agreed. "That's fine. We will find something else. So, Mr. Carter, are you ready to be a Long Horn?"

JC looked at Cobra. Cobra nodded his head to show approval. JC shook the man's hand and asked where to sign. JC could not believe how well his life was going. In just a few weeks' time, he had ruined his scholarship, pushed away the one person that truly cared about him, learned that his coach was just another bloodsucker looking for his payday, and was beat and kicked out of his house by his mother with no explanation. The next day he had a house, a new scholarship, and most importantly to him family!

JC returned to school not at all fazed by the previous drama. He was walking through the halls with a smile. Everyone walked on eggshells, not knowing what to expect. JC went to the locker room to get ready for practice.

Finally one of his teammates broke the silence. "JC, are you all right, bro?"

JC put his hands on the young man's shoulders, took a deep breath, and said, "Bro, I couldn't be better. Life is great."

His teammate was so confused. "But, JC, we heard all about what happened at your house and with your mom's, bro. Are you sure you ain't ready to kill nobody?"

JC smiled and said, "You know what? I am ready to kill somebody." Everyone's eyes got big, and they began to look at each other. "I'm ready to kill somebody on this court, so bring ya butt out here. I feel like dunking on people."

His team was relieved that they were not about to be victims of a homicide. But they still weren't happy that JC felt like dunking on people as they argued amongst each other about who was going to guard him. While they were warming up for practice, his teammate asked, "Hey, JC, who are you staying with?"

JC said with immense pride, "I stay with myself. I'm grown!"

This poor child really thinks that he is being blessed. Why wouldn't he? He prayed to God and everything got better. Or did it? Well it sure seems like it did. He has a house, a car, money, a scholarship, and a family. All of these things seem like such blessing. But just like Granny said, "Everything that glitter ain't gold."

Here is my beef. I can't get past the fact that from a Christian standpoint, gangs and rappers are doing so much better of a job of gathering our people than we are. Cobra did everything that a pastor or a just a child of God should have done for JC—except sending the girls to the house, that is. The only difference is the motive. How long will we sit back and simply talk about how gangs, violence, and music are taking our babies from us? When will we take a stand and say that the streets can't have this child 'cause I'm going to love them and support them and give them another choice? I'm not going to just tell them how bad they are or judge them for taking what they can get.

When I worked in a juvenile detention center, it broke my heart to see the issues that these children came in with. Yes, some of them just wanted to do their own thing, but there were so many kids that just didn't know anything different. How can you expect a child to choose something different when there are no other options presented to them?

Chapter 5

When It Rains, It Pours

Sometimes you feel like you are on top of the world, then you wake up and the world is on top of you. Life can hit you so hard and so fast. You feel like you take one step forward only to be knocked three steps back. Just simply one of those days where you feel like things couldn't get any worse, and then you turn around only to find out your situation has worsened tremendously. Does anyone know what I'm talking about? It's times like these that people will tell you, "Oh, just pray about it, and it will be all right." That is so easy to say when everything is going good in life. Even though they are telling you the truth, you get mad 'cause that same person that told you to just pray about it will claim they are having a nervous breakdown or attempt suicide. Don't you just want to go slap them and say, "Wait a minute. Didn't you tell me to just pray about it? What happened to 'God can fix everything'?" It's a shame that we make the Savior that is oh so real seem so fake. It's in our darkest storm that God can show his true glory.

Tomika had not been to work in days. Her job had been calling, but she had ripped the phone out the wall. Erin, one of Tomika's supervisors, decided to go and check on her. Tomika had not missed a day of work since she had started working. Erin pulled up to the house and rang the doorbell. After no answer, she knocked on the door. It opened when she knocked, so she stepped in, calling Tomika's name. There was no answer and the house was a mess, so Erin began to search the house for Tomika. As she walked in the bathroom, she found Tomika lying lifeless on the floor with an empty bottle of medication in her hand and multiple slashes on her wrist. Tomika had overdosed on pills. Erin called 911 and began CPR on her. "Tomika can you hear me?" she shouted.

Erin checked for a pulse and to see if she was breathing. She found the faintest of heartbeats, and she was barely breathing. Erin rode with her in the ambulance and stayed in the waiting room while she was operated on. The doctor came out and let her know that if she had been brought in a minute later, she would have died. She missed all her major arteries with the cutting, so they just bandaged her wounds. They pumped her stomach and were holding her in ICU until a bed was ready.

Erin thanked the doctor and asked if she could be seen. The doctor said that she was resting and didn't need a lot of company, but Erin ensured that she would be no trouble at all. The doctor smiled and said that he would get the nurses to bring her some pillows and blankets. Erin never left her side. She prayed over Tomika and read scriptures the entire night.

Tomika woke up the next morning to find Erin asleep in a chair next to her bed. Tomika had no idea where she was. The nurse walked in to check on her. Tomika asked the young nurse, "What am I doing here?"

The young lady looked at her and spoke in a very calm voice. "Ms. Carter, you overdosed on medication and where rushed to the ER. That amazing lady right there saved your life. She brought you in and hasn't left your side since you got here. You have an amazing friend. I wish I had someone that cared about me like that."

When the nurse closed the door, Erin woke up. "Oh my God, Tomika, are you all right? You scared me half to death."

All Tomika could say was why. "I don't understand. Why did you come get me? Why did you do that? Why? Why?" After each *why*, the tears flowed harder.

Erin grabbed her hand and began to hug her. "I was so scared, Tomika. You missed work and that wasn't like you. So I came to your house to check on you, and I found you lying there. I thought you were dead. I'm so happy that you are okay."

Tomika began to push Erin away. "But the voice said that no one would care and no one would miss me, and I should just do it. I don't understand! I don't understand!"

Erin tried to calm her down, but Tomika just became irate and demanded for her to go. So Erin grabbed her purse and began to walk out. "Okay, Tomika, I'm going to leave. I will come back later. Just let me pray for you before I go." Erin placed her hand on Tomika's leg and began to pray. "Dear God, please touch this woman's heart and mind. Lord, I don't know what's going on, but I know that you can fix it. There is nothing too hard for you, God. I pray you give her peace and rest, sweet King. Give her the peace that passes all understanding. Thank God. Amen."

Erin then left as promised. Tomika felt a peace that she had not felt since she was a child. She couldn't explain it, but more than that, she could not ignore it.

JC was loving life. He had given his apology in a small press conference and, later that evening, had a meeting with Nike about a shoe endorsement. Everything that Cobra said was going to happen for him was happening. While JC was playing Madden, he received a text telling him that his mother was in the hospital. His heart stopped. He had not talked to his mom since he walked out the house. He jumped in his car and raced to the hospital. All he could think about was that night. He hadn't called her or checked on her. Guilt was overwhelming him. He ran in the doors and asked where her room was. He got off the elevator and stood right outside his mother's door.

Just as he was getting ready to walk in, he thought about all that had happen. He remembered his mom beating him and throwing him out. The guilt that he previously felt was overthrown by the pain and anger he felt for what she had said and done to him. JC wiped his eyes and walked away.

At that very moment, all Tomika could think about was JC. Her one wish was to know that he was okay and to tell him sorry for what she had done. Little did she know her son was only a few steps away.

JC stormed out the hospital and drove home. JC began to reason with himself. "If she don't want me, then I don't want her. She hasn't called me once to even see if I was alive, so why should I care if she is all right? She can die for all I care!"

JC had to do something to get his mind off this. Instead of finding his refuge on the court, he decided to search for it in a party. He called over as many people as he could. Word spread fast. By 7:00 p.m., JC's house was full of people he didn't even know. But he didn't care; he was going to drink and party his problems away. It wasn't very long before JC went on the prowl looking for a young lady to prey on. He grabbed a young lady by the hand and asked her to dance. After dancing they sat in the corner of the room for a second, talking. As they were talking, JC was approached by four guys. One of them boldly stated, "Hey, that's my girl you talking to."

JC said, "Oh really? Well, don't worry. I'm not gonna take her from you for long. I'm just gonna hit it and then you can have her back."

The angry boyfriend grabbed JC and asked, "What the hell did you just say to me?"

JC was well past drunk and repeated his previous statement louder with no hesitation. "I said I'm not gonna take her from you. I'm just gonna hit it and then I will give her back to you."

For the young man, there were no more words to be said. He and his three friends proceeded to give JC the beating of a lifetime. Needless to say, a brawl broke out. It didn't matter if you were a male or a female; if you were standing, you were in danger of being hit. If you were on the floor, you were in danger of being stomped. So the rest of the less-violent people rapidly vacated the house.

JC's house was a mess. Broken TVs, furniture, and windows were everywhere. People began to take parting gifts as well. JC was laid out cold in the middle of his living room floor. He woke up shortly after to see the damage that was caused. When he got to his feet, he saw a big figure standing at the door. He stumbled closer to see who it was. It was Cobra, and he was far from happy about what had happened.

Cobra sat JC on the couch and asked him, "Who did this to you?"

JC replied, "I don't know they names, but I know they faces."

Cobra punched the wall out of frustration and said, "All right, young blood, tomorrow you gonna find them, and when you do, them lil punks is mine. You go get in the car. You are gonna stay with me tonight." Cobra walked over to his crew and demanded that they get the place cleaned up. "Now look, JC, I know you pissed. But don't do nothing stupid. If you do find these fools, you let me handle it. You got too many other thangs to worry about. The last thang I need is for you to be in trouble wit the law or for you to be locked up wit some fools that don't know or care what I would do to them if they touched a hair on your head. You hear me, young blood?"

JC looked up at Cobra and said, "Yeah, I hear ya."

The next day, JC was on a mission. He was determined to find the fools that had jumped him. No one was saying a word about what had happen the previous night. Normally people would be shouting from the rooftops about the beating in belief it helped their street cred. But no one wanted a single bit of cred for crossing Cobra! JC drove around all day trying to catch a glimpse of the faces of his targets, but he had no luck. Even people he remembered being at the party quickly denied being there.

He approached two guys standing outside the movies. He was positive that they were at the party last night. As he walked up, the two young men attempted hard to avoid eye contact. JC walked up with a cocky smirk on his face and said, "So how did you boys like the party last night?"

One of the young men replied, "Man, we wasn't nowhere near yo house last night, so don't come over here with that BS."

JC laughed and said, "Well, that's strike one. Let me ask differently. Who jumped me last night?"

The boy exclaimed again that he had no idea what JC was talking about.

"Strike two!" JC shouted sarcastically. "Now I'm gonna give ya'll one last chance. What were their names?" The young man firmly stated that he didn't know anything. JC yelled, "And you're out! Let's have a recap of this ugly strike out, shall we? Strike one is the fact that I didn't tell you where the party was. Strike two is the fact that I beat ya boi in Madden about four times, so I remember him. The third and final strike is that you are dumb enough to steal my hat and shoes when they clearly have my name stitched in the back and the tongue. So you have a choice. You can either help me find these fools, or I can call Cobra right now and let him know that I found who stole the shoes and hat he had made for me."

They immediately accepted the first option. JC had established his own search party in a matter of minutes. While JC was driving, he remembered that during the very brief conversation they had while dancing, the girl said that she saw him almost every Friday at her job. The only place that he went every Friday night was Jack in the Box on Washington Street. He was in love with their curly fries and tacos.

JC walked into the restaurant and sat down. He waited almost an hour to see if she showed her face. JC had given up. But as he was walking to his car, the young lady was being dropped off. She stepped out of the car and closed the door. When she looked up, she saw JC and her heart stopped. JC walked toward her with a sinister smirk. He looked in the car and saw just the man he was looking for. The young girl was paralyzed with fear. It seemed as if everything was going in slow motion. She mustered up the composure to scream, "Leave now, Mike. He's coming."

The scream startled him as he asked, "Angela, what's wrong?" Mike looked out the window to see who he was. He then stepped out the car and walked straight to JC. "Well, well, well. If it ain't the superstar that thinks he is better than the rest of the world. How is your head feeling?" JC's nostrils flared as he stood face-to-face with his attacker. It seemed Mike had let his pride get the best of him as he taunted JC. "You ready to get yo head busted again?"

JC remembered the words of Cobra and stepped back. "Naw, I'm not gonna fight you. I'm just gonna sit back and watch what Cobra do to you."

Mike did not like that at all. "I knew you was a baby when I first saw you. You got to have someone else fight your battles."

JC defended himself, screaming, "Ain't nobody got to fight my battles. Cobra just said not to waste my time on you and that he would handle my light work." JC pulled his phone out to call Cobra. By this time, they had drawn a major crowd, and the manager had called the police.

Mike pushed JC and told him, "That's right. Call ya daddy so he can save his lil baby."

JC quickly pushed back, stating, "I'm a grown man. I don't need nobody to save me."

"Well, if you such a big man then put the phone down and show me. That is if you ain't afraid that yo daddy gonna whup you. Awww or do you need to call your daddy to save you from your mommy? I heard she stomped dat tail better than I did."

JC lost all control and began to thrash Mike. Punch after punch crashed into Mike's face. JC picked him up and smashed his head into the car window. People stood quiet as JC beat Mike nearly to death. The only thing that kept JC from killing the young man was the cop that came and tackled JC before he could land the fatal blow. As the cops dragged him off, he just kept shouting, "Who's a baby now, huh! Who's a baby now?" It wasn't until the cop car drove away that JC realized what he had done. He put his head against his knee and whispered to himself, "Oh my god!"

Have you ever had that point in your life where it seemed like life couldn't get any better on Monday but life couldn't get worse on Tuesday? JC was doing so well. He had everything that he thought he wanted. Tomika is in a bad place. Or is she? I know that you have heard all the old sayings. It has to get worse before it gets better. It's always the darkest right before the dawn. No pain no gain. As wack as all these statements may be to you, they do hold a great amount of truth. Speaking from personal experience, sometimes God will humble you before he delivers you. At times, I had to be broken down to my lowest point before I would even call to him. Think about it. Who asks for help when they are doing well? Who goes to the doctor for medicine when they feel healthy? It's sad, but we don't want to reach out to God until we are flat on our face.

Chapter 6

Interventions

I remember when I was in middle school; I had a teacher that was racist. She was making my life a living hell. She lied on me, she gave me eighth-grade work in the sixth grade, and worst of all, her actions led to me hearing my grandfather tell me that he was ashamed of me. I had lost hope. I was getting in trouble every week for things I couldn't explain. No one believed me, and I felt so alone. I had made up in my mind that if I was going to do the time, then I might as well do the crime. It was at this time my counselor and my coach came to me and asked me, "What was going on?" When I told them, they didn't just look at me like I told them the dog ate my homework. They investigated and found out I was telling the truth. I don't know what happened to that teacher, but if she ever reads this, I would like to say thank you for all you did to me. It made me better. As for my coach and counselor, I thank God for using them to save my life. If it wasn't for them, I might be on the other side of that detention center door when it closed.

"What have I done? What have I done? God, why did you let this happen to me? What am I gonna do?" All JC could do was ask why and what. He sat in the intake room at the juvenile detention center with his head against the desk as he stared at the floor. The detention officer attempted to get JC's information, but JC was completely unresponsive. He was simply out of it. His heart felt like he had hit a brick wall going a hundred miles an hour. Nothing mattered at this moment. Nothing made sense to him. He was completely numb to the world. The officers made one last attempt to gather his information, but JC was in a daze. Finally, they gave up and sent him to the back.

The officer that was dealing with JC was named Chris. He took JC to the room and told him to take off his clothes and put them in a bag. JC complied and walked to the shower in a zombielike state. Chris walked him to the shower and explained the procedures. "Here is your soap, your shampoo, your towel, and your underwear. You have five minutes to shower. On second thought, you might need to take a little longer than that with all that blood. Tell you what, I will come back in about fifteen minutes—okay, Mr. Julian?"

JC didn't really get it. "My name is JC, and why are you telling me you will be back?"

Chris laughed. "Okay, JC, this must be your first time here, huh. I have to lock you in here, and I come let you out later." It was at that very moment that JC snapped back to reality. As he turned around, the door closed and locked, and JC knew he was no longer free. As the water poured from the showerhead, JC watched the blood swirl in the drain. He continued to have flashbacks of all the events that had led him to this point. *How could I have been so stupid? What the hell was I thinking?* JC was trying to find some explanation for his actions.

Chris came as promised to let JC know he had two minutes left in the shower. JC dried off and put on his underwear and slippers. Chris opened the door and checked the shower for any contraband or illegal objects. He began to walk JC back to his cell, and the chatter began. One of the kids raced to his window to see who the new guy was. "Hey, I know you. Say, everybody, J. Carter in here."

It began an immediate uproar. "What J. Carter? The basketball player? I hate that punk! Wait till I get a hold of you. Cobra ain't gonna save you in here."

Threats continued to pour out for the next couple of seconds until Chris shouted, "Hey. Are you serious? Ya'll just gonna disrespect me like I'm not here. Cut out all that cursing and actin' a fool. Ya'll know better than that."

JC looked at Chris with a skeptical eye as if to say "Do you really think that's gonna work?" But much to JC's surprise, Chris's words were well taken, and several of the kids gave sincere apologies. "Man, I'm sorry, Chris. Our bad."

Chris escorted JC into his cell and said, "Wow, you are definitely the most disliked person I have ever seen come into this place. You even got Mouse crunk back there, and he don't hardly ever say a word unless he trying to make someone laugh. I see now that this is going to be a long stay for you."

Chris closed the door and left the hall. It only took a few seconds for the boys to get to their doors and start the newbie interrogation. "Say, J. Carter, what you in here for?" one of the kids quickly inquired.

"That's none of ya biz, dude. I'm gonna mind mine and you mind yours," JC replied.

"Naw, see, that's where you wrong. Everything that happens here is my biz. I'm Noel. I'm the OG in A hall. This the last time I'm gonna ask you nicely. 'Cause Chris ain't gonna be here to save you always. So what you in here for?"

JC is clearly known for a smart mouth, so his next statement came with no thought. "Okay, I'll tell you. They arrested me for slappin' ya mama 'cause she tried to hold out on the money she made boppin' on Ninth Street."

The only words to explain the events after that were complete and utter chaos. It was almost amazing to hear the combination of violent and vulgar language that went forth in A hall that night. These kids were saying things that would make Bernie Mac blush. All detention officers were called to A hall to get the kids under control. There were only fifteen cells on A Hall, but the noise was equivalent to a war scene off the movie *300* nd maybe a little more violent. Needless to say, JC wasted no time turning a bad situation into the worst with nothing but the opening of his mouth.

Three hours, sixty-three articles of discipline, six restraints, and nine twenty-four-hour confinements later, the hall was quiet. The superintendent was called in to find out what was gonna be done with Julian James Carter. The superintendent had no concern with JC. "We will treat him like any other kid that comes through the facility," one of the supervisors quickly replied.

"Sir, but you don't understand what has happened here. I have been working her for twenty-five years. I've seen the most violent of violent kids. I seen thieves, rapists, and murderers come through this place. But I have never seen a child walk in these doors and cause the hell that this boy caused without ever leaving his room."

The supervisor might as well have been talking to a wall because the superintendent was unwavering in his judgment. "Deal with him. I'm going home!"

There was a team meeting in the control room about their new guest. "Does anybody have any ideas?"

Chris raised his hand. "We can clear C hall and put him in there. That will at least keep him from stirring up any more trouble while they are in their rooms. As far as bringing him out to the dayroom, I have no ideas whatsoever. The second these kids see him, they are gonna beat his head in.

Even Mouse was threatening this guy, and you know he loves everybody. Let me go to A hall, find out why they hate him so much."

Kayla, one of the DOs, said, "Let me save you the trouble. They hate him 'cause he is a BUTT HOLE. That is Julian Carter. That's the kid that showed up drunk to his press conference and told everybody to go to hell and buy his shoes."

"Naw, it's got to be more than that," Chris replied. "I'll find out what it is. Until then, we will put him in C Hall."

After JC was transferred to C hall, Chris entered back into the belly of the beast to talk to his kids. "Look, fellas, I don't know what just happened, but I need ya'll to let me know what is going on. Talk to me. Somebody. Mouse, you tell me."

Mouse was a fifteen-year-old boy. He was in JDC for drug charges. He was a good kid that was always good for a laugh and was cool with everybody. Mouse walked to his door, and Chris opened it. "Have a seat on your bed, Mouse, and tell me what's going on."

Mouse sat on his bed and began to explain. "Man, Chris, everybody hate that dude. He is Cobra's golden boy. He walks around like he is God. One day when I was at school, I was walking with my sister and a couple of her homegirls. We were having lunch and JC walked up. He told them that he was gonna be bored tonight and he wanted some company and wanted them to come over that night. I spent all day telling them not to go, but they just kept talking about how fly JC was and how cute he was and how lucky they were to get asked by him. Anyways, when they got there, no one was there but JC. He got them drunk and started messing with them and getting them to take their clothes off. When he got to my sister, she said that she didn't want to do it, so he grabbed her, ripped off her bra and underwear, and pushed her out the door and told her that girls don't tell him no. So she could get the hell out. She had to walk all the way home naked and crying her eyes out. I will never forget her face when she came through the door. I told some of my homeboys about it, but they were too scared to do anything 'cause Cobra put the word out that anybody that touches him will have to deal with him. I want to kill him, Chris. I want to kill him! I want to kill him!"

Chris calmed the young man down and closed his door. It seemed that every boy in A hall had a female close to them that was done wrong or was taken advantage of by JC. The sad thing was B hall didn't even know he was there yet. They might have all felt the same way.

The next day, JC was kept in his room. The day-shift staff lacked the manpower or desire to deal with the drama that was promised if JC was allowed to enter the dayroom. When Chris came back to work the next day, Johnny, his supervisor, approached him and let him know that they were planning to let Carter out at free time. Chris was quick to ask what staff was working that day. "I need to know who is all here, sir."

John looked at the schedule and began to read off the names. "We got you, Kayla, Holley, Mike, Shawn, Kyle, Steve, and JW."

Chris took a deep breath and said, "Okay, boss. We can give it a shot."

The name that really stood out for him was JW. JW and Chris were the most respected DOs (detention officers) in the facility. They had an amazing relationship with the kids and seemed to always be able to deescalate the situation if possible and handle the physical side if it came to it. Chris saw JW as a father figure at the job. The kids would make jokes and refer to Chris and JW as Pops and Grandpa. Chris went into the control room to set out the game plan. A lot of the other workers didn't like Chris and JW's methods, but they couldn't argue with the results. But some were simply there for the money and power of the job and to be able to control and affect the kids' lives. These were the people that always bumped heads with the two of them. If there was one thing that JW and Chris didn't stand for, it was the kids being mistreated.

Chris cleared his throat and got everybody's attention. "Look, after last night, we all know that this is gonna be a crazy day. We are gonna split up the free time. A hall will come out first, and B hall will come out last. We are going to bring JC out with B hall. If anything looks fishy, then pack them up and put them in their room right then. We have to stay on our toes today."

Holley rudely added, "I didn't know that you were the new supervisor. You coming in here barking orders like you are in charge!"

Chris gave no attention to Holley's comment. "All right, everybody, let's make it happen," Chris stated with a smile.

Holley's intentions at the job were very clear. She was on a power trip. It didn't help that she was extremely attention-starved and desired to be accepted by others. This was especially true regarding her low self-esteem and misguided need to feel sexy. She often flirted with the kids in an attempt to boost her wounded ego. She even went as far as to act on some of her flirtatious comments with the juveniles. The kids hated her and always complained of her baiting them into trouble or blatantly lying on them. She spent much of her time causing problems that other workers had to clean up. The previous week, she had caused two kids to be put on twenty-four-hour confinement because she gave them an article of discipline for not returning a flirtatious action that she initiated toward them. The kids were furious and tried to explain, but Holley simply cut them off and forced the supervisor to back her up. "Are you just gonna take the word of the kids over your staff? I thought that we were a team?" she asked as if she was being victimized.

The supervisor knew that he must protect his staff, so he enforced the punishment she had handed out. She then looked at the young men and blew them a kiss with a wink. She was a thorn in everyone's side, but no one had decided to deal with her yet. Chris had seen less serious cases of this behavior from Holley and always made sure it was dealt with. This was one of the reasons that Chris and Holley didn't see eye to eye. Chris always found a tactful way to override Holley's bogus discipline. It was as if he was robbing her of the one joy she had at the job.

Chris could tell that Holley was going to try something today. She had that vindictive look in her eye. The rest of the staff began to prepare to let the kids out. After everyone was seated at the dayroom, it was completely silent. That was never a good thing. The only time the kids were quiet without being told was when they were eating, sleeping, or when a good movie was on.

JW sensed the calm before the storm and stood at the front of the dayroom to call for everyone's attention. "Good evening, ladies and gentlemen. I heard that ya'll had quite the party while I was gone last night. You know that I don't like to dwell on the past, but I'm gonna do that for a sec. That mess that happened last night will not happen anymore, or I will personally see that you don't come out of your rooms until it snows."

One of the kids quickly added, "But, Grandpa, it's almost summer and it don't ever snow here."

JW looked up with a cocky grin and said, "I know! So if you want to wait until you can build snowmen on the court before you see it again, then have another episode like last night. Do I make myself clear?"

"Yes, sir!" the kids answered in unison. It only took a few minutes before one of the kids inquired to the absence of JC.

Drew motioned for Chris to come to his table. "Hey, Pops, where J. Carter at?"

Chris gave him a look that clearly said, "Do you think you need to be asking that?"

Drew picked up on the hint. "All right, Pops, I will shut up."

The current silence was much too boring for Holley, so she began her usual false accusations to stir up the kids and bait them into losing their cool. "Ya'll quit leaning back in your chairs," she shouted. Chris saw the kids about to fall right into the trap, and before the young men could respond, Chris sternly shouted, "Mark and Mike, what did I tell you?"

The two young men looked over to him, looked at Holley, took a deep breath, nodded their heads, and kept silent. Chris had been talking to the kids about keeping their cool. He was well aware of Holley's intent but knew that if he could get the kids not to respond, then he could keep them out of trouble.

Holley was not happy with the respect the kids showed JW and Chris. She was even less happy with her failed attempt to start some drama. She gave Chris a salty stare and he replied back with a Kool-Aid smile and thumbs-up and sarcastically stated, "Don't worry, Holley, I got your back."

JW and the other DOs simply covered their mouths and laughed. The bad blood between Holley and Chris was no secret.

Chris walked down B hall to go make his rounds. As soon as he stepped down the hall, one of the kids yelled, "Hey, it's Chris, ya'll." Everyone ran to the door, calling for him to come talk to them.

"How are my boys doing today?"

Kenny, one of the older kids, called Chris over to his door with a big smile on his face. "Dang, Pops, we thought you forgot about us. We ain't seen you at all last night. So what's up? You didn't even come and pray with us last night. You don't ever forget to pray with us."

Chris continued to do his door checks. "You right, Kenny, I don't ever forget to pray with ya'll. But ya'll was asleep when I came and prayed. I didn't leave till three in the morning."

"All right, Pops, just making sure you don't forget about us."

Chris laughed. "Now do you think I would forget about my boys? Ya'll be good. I will be back."

Kenny quickly shouted, "Wait, are we gonna get to come out for our free time today?"

Chris turned back and stated, "Now you know that depends on how ya'll act."

Chris then went to check on the most famous visitor of them all. When he walked into C hall, he heard JC talking. "You can't hold me! I'm gonna blow right by you. I told you, you can't hold me. I'm a monster. Get back. That's my rebound. Get ya weight up, boy."

Chris walked to the door to find JC in the third quarter of his imaginary game of basketball. He looked in and said, "Hey, you should take that guy to the left. That back foot looks a lil shaky."

JC looked back to the door and went to sit on the bed.

"Don't stop, JC. I want to see how the game ends."

JC gave a displeased expression and stated, "Are you done patronizing me, officer?"

Chris looked shocked. "Patronizing? Well, I see we have some book smarts in that head of yours. I hope you have some common sense to accompany it. Look, JC, I'm not here to give you a hard time. I find no happiness in your misery. Whether you believe it or not, I'm here to help you."

JC quickly walked to the door. "Oh, you are here to help me. What the hell was I thinking? And all this time I thought that you was here to keep me locked in this box. Okay, you want to help. How about this. Go to hell! That will really help. I don't want a thang from any of you bastards, so don't say nothing to me and I will return the favor. Thank you so much, Mr. Chris."

Chris just smiled. "Well, I'm glad to see you are having a better day, Mr. JC. I will be back a lil later to get some info from you." He walked out calmly and returned to the dayroom.

JC lay on his bed, staring at the wall and talking to himself. "I'm gonna go crazy in here. Everyone in this place wants to beat my brains out, and I'm sure that these dirty officers are just gonna let it happen. Why can't I keep my freakin' mouth shut?" As JC was looking at the wall, he closed his eyes and said, "God, what do I do now?"

At that moment, a voice said clearly, "Get up and get dressed."

JC jumped up from his bed, looking around the room, and said, "God? Is that you?"

The voice replied back, "No, it's Kayla. Chris said to get your clothes on and he will be in to get you in about five minutes." It was the intercom in his room.

JC got dressed and waited. Chris came promptly as promised. He opened JC's door and asked him to have a seat on his bed. JC sat and put his head in his hands. "Well, JC, I'm gonna need you to finish giving me your info so I can get you in the system and get a hold of your parents."

JC had not thought once about his mom since he had left the hospital that day. JC's entire demeanor changed. "Will you let me call my mom if I give you all my info?"

"Why, yes, sir, I will," Chris replied.

JC quickly answered every question asked. "Okay, I answered all you questions. Can I make that call now?"

Chris began to explain to him, "Well, I can't let you call right now. You will have to wait until visitation time."

JC quickly asked when that would be, and he was informed that it would begin at 7:00 p.m.

"Are you ready to come out for free time today?"

JC looked up and, without thinking, yelled, "Hell no. I'm not trying to get killed out there. Just come get me when I can make that call."

"Well, okay, Mr. JC. I will do that."

Seconds felt like minutes, minutes like hours, and hours like days. Finally seven o'clock had rolled around, and JC heard the door open to C hall and quickly ran to see who it was. Chris came as promised. He opened JC's door and escorted him to the phones. JC explained to Chris that his mother had been in the hospital and wouldn't be able to be reached at her number. Chris walked into the control room and made a phone call to the hospital to inquire the room number of Tomika Carter. After making the connection, he gave JC the heads-up and told him to pick up the phone. There were a few moments of silence as they listened to each other breathe.

Erin walked over to Tomika, firmly grasped her hand, and softly whispered, "Say something, baby. Don't just sit there."

Tomika squeezed Erin's hand tight, closed her eyes and exhaled, then mustered out, "Well, hello, son. How are you doing?"

JC immediately burst into tears. "Mama, I'm sorry. I'm so, so sorry! I should've been there with you."

Tomika quickly followed suit, shedding her own downpour of tears, "No, I'm sorry, baby. I should've never put you out. Then neither one of us would be in this position. I should be out of the hospital in about three or four days, and I will come to visit you as soon as I can. I've got somebody for you to meet. JC, please don't cause any trouble for yourself."

"C'mon, Mom, now you know me," JC replied.

"That's exactly why I'm telling you not to cause any trouble for yourself."

Chris gave JC the sign that his time was up.

"Okay, Mom, I have to get off the phone. You promise you going to come?"

"I promise, baby," Tomika answered. Tomika took a deep breath, a hard swallow, and uttered three words that left her son emotionally paralyzed, "I love you."

The floodgates opened from JC's eyes once again as he mustered out, "I love you too, Mommy." JC hung up the receiver and began to walk briskly back to C hall, attempting to hide his tears from the rest of the DOs. Chris stormed out the control room to catch up with him and escort him back to his room. JC dove onto his bed, burying his face in his pillow.

As he continued to cry, Chris attempted to offer some words of comfort. "You know if you need to talk, I'm here, right?"

JC ignored his offering and continued to cry. Chris was respectful to the young man's unspoken wishes as he walked out and let him know that the offer still stands. JC could not make sense of the events that just transpired. *Did she really just say she loved me? Did she really say I was her baby?* These words of endearment had been desired but were so unobtainable for most of his life. He could not remember the last time his mother had referred to him as her baby or told him that she loved him. No matter how hard or strong he tried to be, no matter how many emotional walls or barricades he had put up to protect his fragile heart, they were all demolished the second those words were uttered.

What made her say this? Why isn't she mad? She didn't even ask me what I did. She just said she was coming. I don't know what this means. JC fell to his knees and looked to the sky as he held his hand over his heart. He was unable to muster out a single word, but somehow he knew for the first time in his life God could hear him.

Chris had made his rounds throughout the rest of the halls and was finishing up the paperwork for the shift change. Just like every night at 10:50, he made his way to A hall. He walked in and said, "All right, boys, close your eyes and bow your heads. Any prayer requests?"

Several kids requested prayer for family members, a couple for their own emotional guidance, and two to simply get out of there. Chris walked up and down the hall with his eyes closed, saying a good night prayer for the kids and beseeching the Lord on their behalf. After the prayer, he walked out as he told the children, "I love ya'll, and I'll see ya'll tomorrow."

They followed with a unanimous "We love you too."

Chris repeated the same actions in B hall as he did every night then made his way to C hall. He found JC still on his knees with his head bowed to the ground. He unlocked his door, walked in, and placed his hand on JC's shoulder. JC was startled and jumped away, backing himself into the wall. Chris walked over to him and did something JC never expected. He stood there with his arms open and said, "Come here."

JC did not understand Chris's actions or his own as he walked into Chris's open arms. JC began to cry harder as Chris began to pray, "Dear God, I praise your holy name. I come to you asking that you forgive me of all my sins. Lord, I pray that you begin to open this young man's heart and provide healing for him. I don't know his pain and I don't know his struggle, but I know that you are the answer. I pray you send your Holy Spirit to dwell with him and give him the peace that passes all understanding. I pray that you allow me to be used to intervene on any attack the enemy places against him. It's in your son Jesus name I pray. Thank God. Amen."

And who said going to jail is a bad thing? Well, I guess it is, or it can be. It's crazy that both Tomika and JC were brought to what seems to be their lowest point. What the devil meant for your bad, God meant for your good because it was at this point they were reachable to people that truly needed the opportunity to show God's grace and love. I think JC might have actually found just the person to show him the error of his ways and introduce him to somebody that can fix all and be all. None other than the son of Mary, King of Kings, Lord of Lords, my savior and yours, Jesus.

Amazingly enough, Tomika has also received her first taste of the unending love of God. Erin is the first person to stand by Tomika's side with no promise of personal gain in sight. Now I know you've seen enough television shows to know that everyone in the position of authority doesn't use that authority right. Hint, hint: Rodney King.

People in authority sometimes feel it's their right to exploit those that they have power over. But the Word lets us know what's done in the dark shall come to the light. For all of you that haven't let go of the judgmental tip yet, don't feed me that junk about doing the crime and paying the time. The purpose of them being locked up is punishment—that is correct. But them being separated from their family and being stripped from most unappreciated freedoms is punishment enough. Nowhere in the Constitution does it say they should be emotionally, physically, or spiritually taken advantage of. I've seen so many good kids go into the system and never be able to escape the mark it leaves. I don't even know why people waste their time calling people ex-con 'cause in your mind they are still cons. They just haven't been caught yet.

Here's my latest memo: To the church and anyone else that considers themselves higher than the thugs, thieves, and miscreants that laid their heads in these facilities, the only difference between you and them is that you didn't get caught. I dare most of you to lie and say that you've never done anything worthy of being locked up in a juvenile detention center. All I am simply saying is these kids should not be the next topic at your church bingo night or the new hot gossip for the over-fifty phone club that never leave their homes and have nothing better to do than talk about whose grandbaby ain't worth nothing today. They should be on top of your prayer list. They should be the first hand that you reach out to grab and pull up. They should be yet another testimony for the glory of God, another lost soul that the saints rejoice over winning in God's name.

So if you feel convicted by the statements I just made, good! Don't get mad; get active. And if all else fails, ask yourself this question: who have you brought closer to Jesus today?

Chapter 7

Re-breaking Bones

Sometimes you have to re-break a bone in order for it to heal right. Either it didn't get the adequate attention the first time or something happened while it was healing and it was never corrected. This goes the same for broken hearts. Sometimes you have to re-break a heart for it to ever work again. So many people go through life emotionally crippled because they lack the courage or trust to deal with the past that has ravaged them their whole life. It takes real love for a person to make it through this. Someone that has the patience, understanding, and guidance to navigate through the sorrows, pains, and tears that lie along this path. As great as the pain may be, once you're healed right, you may only remember the path and not the pain. God seems to work this way.

"Erin, you were so right. I just trusted and prayed for God to let me talk to my son. I can't explain it, but I knew it was going to happen."

Erin smiled at Tomika's comment. "Now you see, ma'am, that is what we call faith. Faith is the substance of things hoped for and the evidence of things not seen. Hebrews 11:1. Tomika, I'm so proud of you."

"Erin, can I ask you something?"

"Why yes, ma'am, you can."

"Erin, why are you here? I was so hateful to you. I made you leave. I never even told you thank-you for saving my life. You've shown me nothing but kindness even before I got in this situation. Please help me understand why you are here."

Erin laughed, "This may make no sense to you, dear, but I'm here because I love you. And the Word tells me that love is unending, love is kind, love is patient, love is not boastful, and love is not proud. So all

I can say is I'm here. I am here because God commands my heart, and he commands my heart with love. So there is your answer, Ms. Tomika Carter. I am here because I love you."

Tomika fell into a blank stare across the room and spoke in a raspy tone, "Do you know how many times I've heard a man tell me he loved me? Do you know how many people have hurt me with those very words? Love leaves you alone at night. Love makes you a homewrecker. Love labels you the town whore. Love gets you a child by a man that wants nothing to do with you. Love hits you in your face when you don't do what it wants you to do. Love leaves you bloody, raped, and bruised on the floor of a fraternity house after initiations are over. This is how I know love. So please don't tell me that you're here for that reason because to be perfectly honest, I'm pretty dang tired of that word."

Erin watched as Tomika rebuilt every wall she had guarded against her heart. She ran to Tomika's bed and firmly grasped her face, bringing them eye-to-eye. With tears pouring down her face, she screamed, "That's a lie! That is not what love is. I know what it's like to have a man tell you that he'll never do it again and that he loves you too much for that. I know what it's like for them to take your innocence and look your mother in the eye and say I love you too much to do that. I know what it's like for them to take every bit of decency you have and wipe their butt with it. And I tell you, ma'am, that ain't what love is. Tomika, I know they've hurt you. I know they've abused you. They did it to me too, baby. But one thing that I know—and it took me fifteen years to find out—but oh, how I know that ain't love. And as God is my witness, I'm going to show you what real love is. Do you hear me? Tomika, do you hear me?"

Tomika looked up like a scorned child and mustered out, "Yes. But I'm scared, Erin. I'm scared."

Chris barely got a stitch of sleep. His heart was overjoyed that JC had came to his humbling point. He spent much of the night praying and thinking of how he could help JC and the other kids. For a long time, Chris had been trying to get his program on its feet. He was not sure of how the kids would take it, but he felt like the time was now. "No more excuses, Chris. These boys need this. Get off yo butt, write the proposal, and take it to the chief. The worse thing he can say is no. And why am I talking to myself?"

Chris jumped out of his bed and ran to the computer to type out his proposal for his class. That day, he showed up to work a couple of hours early so he could speak with the chief.

It's funny how God works. He'll often put the same idea on other people's hearts. JW so happened to be at the detention center early that day as well. As Chris got out of his car, he yelled across the parking lot, "Hey, Pops, you know they don't give overtime, right? What you doin' here so early?" JW just laughed.

Chris jogged over to greet his father figure with a handshake and hug. "I should be saying the same to you, boy. What you doin' at work so early?"

"I asked you first, Pops." JW looked back to see if anyone else was around. "I couldn't sleep last night, Chris. I just kept thinking about the boys and my daughter. Somebody has to teach these boys how to be a man. Out of all the boys we got in there, maybe five of them have a man present, and probably only two of them have any type of positive figure in their life, period. Boys are raising boys, Chris, and this world don't care."

Chris just stood there with a Kool-Aid smile. "You know the Lord works in mysterious ways. I had the same problem last night, and I think you just may be the answer to my prayers, Pops. I'm about to go present my class to the chief."

"Now, Chris, you know I'm all for education and it's great, but these boys need to be taught how to be men."

"I know, Pops. That's exactly what the class will teach. It's called From Boys to Gentlemen. It's a class teaching young boys how to become respectful and successful young men. The mission statement for the class is the wise words of the late great Clemmie D."

"Your grandfather?" JW asked.

Chris replied with a smile, "The one and only. He always taught me to treat a woman like you want your mama, your sister, or your daughter to be treated. I got a lot of different discussions and school type curriculum to give the boys, and I thought if it was certified by the chief, it's something that the boys could use in court as a rehabilitation tool."

JW grabbed Chris, picked him up, and yelled with extreme excitement, "Ha ha. That's my boy! That is amazing!"

"Now you better be careful before you throw your back out, old man. Put me down. You ain't twenty no more. You ain't thirty either. Wait, you ain't forty. Man, you ain't even fifty." JW laughed at Chris's smart comments. "Do you really think this a good idea, Pops?"

JW gave no verbal response. He walked to the door, opened it, and said, "What are you waiting for? We have a class for you to present."

Chris and JW walked in to meet with the chief along with the superintendant. "JW, Chris, what can I do for you?"

"Well, sir, I'll get straight down to business. I have a class that I would like to present to you for the boys." He laid the proposal down on the desk. The chief carefully read over the proposal. He placed the paper on the desk and looked at the two gentlemen and said, "I only have two questions. One, are you sure you want to do this?"

Chris looked at JW, and JW gave a nod of approval. "With all of my heart, sir," Chris replied.

The chief then said, "Well, I only have one other question. When can you start?"

Chris eagerly responded, "Today."

The superintendant pulled out his pen and signed the proposal to show his approval, and the chief followed suit. The chief explained, "Follow guidelines in the JPA (Juvenile Protective Act) and you have my full backing. Congratulations."

Chris and JW were overjoyed. "Pops, this is really happening."

Julian placed his hand on Chris's shoulder. "Look, let me lay down the law right now. I'm here for support! All that class stuff, that's all on you. Hell, you never know—you'll probably teach me a couple of things. So get your little smooth-talking tail in there and learn these kids something about how to be a man."

Chris looked back with a smile and said, "You sound just like my grandpa."

JW smiled and said, "Well, I think I'll take that as a compliment."

Chris went into Johnny's office to show him the proposal for his class and to work out the scheduled dates. Looking from the outside in, it may have seemed a little cocky for Chris to start scheduling dates without confirming it with the kids first, but truth be told, the kids would sign up for corn-shucking classes as long as Chris was teaching it. It was simply one of those things that you either loved and respected about Chris or hated and found yourself extremely envious of.

Once the kids were brought out to the dayroom, JW stood at the front and made the daily announcements. At the end, JW turned over the floor to Chris to announce his class. "Ladies and gentlemen, starting tomorrow, I will be administering a class. It is completely optional. The name of the class is called From Boys to Gentlemen. Anyone that is interested can come sign up as your name is called. The class for you, ladies, has not been prepared yet but will come at a later date. Thank you for your cooperation and have an amazing detention center day."

Every young man in the facility signed the paper except for one. Let me give you a hint: first name starts with a J, last name starts with a C. Our little rebel was uninterested from the moment it was made optional. Needless to say, Chris received a mixed reaction from his coworkers. Some thought it was a great idea and couldn't wait to support it. Others, a.k.a. Holley, saw it as unnecessary and pointless. After the first free time, there was a small meeting in the control room. Chris cleared his throat and stated, "Well, ladies and gentlemen, I'll make this short and sweet. It's been on my heart to do this class for a long time, but now it's becoming such a need that I feel led to act on it. I will be doing the class three times a week and will welcome any positive input given or constructive criticism offered. I truly believe this class can make a difference in these boys' lives, and for those of you that could care less, it will make your jobs a lot easier."

Right on time, Holley jumped in with a discouraging comment for the day. "Well, I can tell you right now it's not gon' work. Most of these boys don't even want to be a gentleman. They're just thugs and drug dealers. That's why they're in here. You'll see. If anything, it will just make things worse."

Chris was almost drawn into responding to Holley's ignorant and hateful words but, once again, remembered who she was. He did what he did best. "So if no one has any positive input or constructive criticism, this meeting is adjourned."

This was the final straw for Holley. She had been outclassed for the last time. If you truly want to piss off an attention-craving person, ignore them. *Chris thinks he's so dang funny. But that's all right. I'll show him*, Holley thought to herself.

The buzz began to spread about the class. As expected, few kids knew what the class was for. They just knew that Chris was teaching it. Chris made his rounds through the halls, and the kids inquired for more info on the Boys to Gentlemen class. "Well, you'll just have to come to the class and find out, won't you?" was his constant reply to all questions. Chris made his way to C hall to check on JC. He approached the door and called the young superstar's name. "What's good with you, JC? How has your day been?"

JC snapped back stating, "You just want me to get my head beat in, don't you? I don't know why I thought you were any different."

Chris stared at JC with the most confused of looks. "Please let me know what you are talkin' 'bout 'cause I have no idea. Where is all this comin' from?"

JC continued to express his displeasure by saying "I was doin' just fine here in the room, hadn't caused any more problems since the other night, but now ya'll are going to make me come out for free time?"

It was official. Chris was totally lost. "Hold on, hold on, hold on. What do you mean make you come out for free time? Who said you had to come out for free time?"

"The superintendant just came and visited me. He said that one of his DOs reported to him that I had refused to come out of my room and that is not acceptable. He said I am to follow all rules and regulations and will not be treated any different from any other juvenile in this facility. And the next time I decide to disrespect one of his staff, my phone and visitation rights will be revoked. Other than the old man that brings me breakfast and lunch, you are the only DO I've talk to in this facility. So thanks for telling the superintendant how you feel about me. Then I get a phone call today from my supposed lawyer. Cobra sent him to give me a message. He said that a hard head makes a soft behind, and since I didn't want to listen and I messed up his money by getting put in here, then he has made me fair game. The only reason I would make it out of here in one piece is because these fools are scared of Cobra. I'm screwed, and you just gonna throw me to the wolves."

Chris was about to make an attempt to defend himself but, at that moment, realized what had happened. "Holley. Look, JC, you are going to have to trust me."

"Oh yeah, like I haven't heard that one a thousand times. You just doin' this cause I didn't want to take that stupid class."

Chris began to get a tad bit agitated and spoke more sternly than he ever had before, "Look, young sir. I know you upset and frustrated with the situation, but I didn't throw any false accusations at you. So show me the same respect. I am going to go find out what's going on. You sit tight and keep quiet. If anybody comes over the intercom asking questions, be respectful. I mean it, lil' boy."

JC jumped up and stated, "Little boy? I'm a grown dang man."

Chris answered quickly saying, "Huh, that's funny. 'Cause we don't allow grown dang people in this facility. That's why they call it the juvenile detention center."

Chris stormed into the control room and walked over to Holley. "Did you go talk to the superintendant about JC?"

"Oh my, do ya'll hear someone talking?" Holley stated with a sinister grin.

Chris then turned around and spoke to the rest of the DOs, "Well, I hope everyone ate their Wheaties today—'cause from what I hear, JC will be coming out his room for the second free time this evening."

Johnny was the first to stand up. "Why the hell you say that? We keepin' him in his room for as long as he'll stay."

Just then the superintendant knocked on the door of the control room. Mike leaned over to Kayla and whispered, "That man don't look happy at all."

The superintendant walked in. "Look, ladies and gentlemen, it's been brought to my attention that this Julian Carter character has been running my facility and not my DOs. Well, that stops now! He comes out the same time as everyone else. He does everything else the same time as everyone else. If ya'll aren't strong enough to handle this juvenile, then maybe I need some new DOs. As far as him disrespecting the female staff, that will stop immediately. The first thing he says inappropriate to any of the female staff is an immediate revoking of all his visitation and phone call privileges. Do I make myself clear?"

Maybe at another time, Chris would sit back and hold his peace. But this was one of the few occasions he was unable to do so. "No, sir, we are not completely clear. My first question is, what female staff did he disrespect? To my knowledge, he hasn't left his room since the night of the major incident except to be showered. Plus, I was the one to escort him to the shower, and he had no verbal contact with any female staff under my watch. So what female staff could he have possibly come in contact with inside his room? They aren't allowed to do door checks on him."

The superintendent was a little baffled by what Chris had presented. "Well, Ms. Holley informed me that he was blatantly disrespectful to her and used profanity towards her in front of several male DOs that she would rather not name."

Chris was persistent with his question. "Sir, I'm not sure you heard me. How can this occur if he never left his room?"

Chris had brought up a fatal flaw in Holley's scheme. The superintendant had no answer for him. "Well, Chris, you don't worry about that. I'll get to the bottom of that. As far as him staying in his room just because he wants to or just because you all are scared? Neither one will be tolerated. Is that understood?"

"Yes, sir, it is," Johnny quickly intervened. The world says, 'A house divided will not stand.' Well if that's true, this house will stand about as long a drunk, one-leg man on roller skates."

Chris attempted to calm the storm that was at hand but was quickly interrupted by Kyle. "Look, Chris, we're not trying to hear one of them after-school special speeches you got for us. We tired of this crap, and I think the crap know exactly who we talking about."

The last thing Holley expected was to be exposed as the mystery informant to the superintendant. Everyone now knew it was her despite her constant denial of the statements. The male staff was frustrated with the accusation of them not protecting the female staff. The remaining female staff were pissed at the picture of them being painted as helpless.

Chris walked over to JW, searching for some advice. "Well, what are we gonna do, Pops?"

JW scratched his head and looked at the disturbed young man. "Hell, I don't know. You think you can make up class for team unity?"

"This ain't funny, Pops. It's really finna be some problems in this place. You know a lot of these kids are up for early release. The last thing they need on their file is an assault charge."

JW paused then said, "You don't think they gon' hit her, do you?"

Chris clarified, saying, "No, Pops, not her! JC."

"Oooohhh. Yeah, I forgot about him. You're right. We are in trouble."

It was time for the second free time. As the kids were out, they could smell the division amongst the DOs, like sharks smelling blood in water. After A hall and B hall were released and seated, Chris went to C hall to retrieve JC. JC looked up and said, "What are you doing?"

Chris lowered his head and said, "You gotta come out, JC. It's out of my hands."

JC put on his jumpsuit, slid on his slippers, and began to walk down C hall to the exit. It seemed like everything was going in slow mode for JC. He felt like a lamb being taken off to the slaughter. Chris could hear JC's heartbeat from three steps behind him. He was escorted to the dayroom and told to have a seat. He must have been playing Tupac because once his feet hit the carpet of the dayroom, all eyes were on him. The murmuring began. The word had definitely got out about JC no longer being under Cobra's protection. It wasn't a question of what was going to happen but simply when.

Some of the more timid juveniles found their way to put as much distance as possible between them and the soon-to-come action. One thing was for sure, none of the kids wanted JW or Chris to be present. One of the older juveniles, Marco, stood up from across the room. He was joined by a fellow juvenile Isaiah. Chris was completely taken aback by this action. It was clear that they were about to fight, but it made no sense. These were two of the most well-behaved young men in the facility. They had not gotten themselves into a stitch of trouble in months.

Chris left JC's side and shouted with a stern voice, "Hey, ya'll sit down. Now!"

They both looked at Chris then back at each other. Marco lowered his head and stated, "I'm sorry, Chris, I hope you still love us after this."

Marco raced toward Isaiah, fist drawn, and the battle began. Of course, Chris and JW were the first to go restrain the young men. While Chris and JW handled the restraints, the rest of the DOs kept the others calm. Chris escorted Marco to his room, and JW escorted Isaiah shortly after. They put up no fight until they reached the room. Once they were in the room, they began to resist heavily. Marco began to kick and twist violently. "I'm sorry, Chris, but I have to do this. I've got to do it. I'm sorry."

Chris stood a whopping five feet seven inches, 185 pounds, while Marco was six feet and a solid 205 pounds. This size difference was of little effect. The determining factor was Chris's "country strength." It was as if he had been steer-wrestling most of his young life. Chris quickly but safely took Marco to the ground. "What do you mean you're sorry? What has gotten into you, boy?"

During the scuffle, the door to the room had been locked. Chris called on his radio for assistance, but little did he know of the turn of events that were transpiring in the dayroom. Chris received no answer on the radio after several attempts. "What the hell is goin on?" Chris said to himself.

Finally JW came over the radio. "Chris, are you there?"

"Yeah, I'm here. Pops, what is goin' on?"

"It was a set-up. The kids didn't want us in the dayroom when they went after JC, so these two staged a fight to get us to take these two to their room. And now we're locked in here."

"Well, who is in the control room? Get on the intercom to see if you can get them to pop the door," Chris ordered.

"All right. I'm on it."

Chris walked over to Marco and took off his cuffs. "Is this true, Marco?"

Marco looked up with streams of tears running from his eyes, "You gotta understand, Chris. They made us do it. They said they was gon' hurt some of our family if we didn't help them get JC. I can't have my family getting hurt behind me. You hate me, don't you? You hate me now!"

Chris was aggravated with the statement. "Boy, shut up. I ain't never gonna hate you, but that ain't the point. I ought to kick you in ya head. But I probably would've did the same thing if I was in yo position." At that time, Chris heard the door lock pop. He raced out the door, down the hall, and back into the dayroom.

JC was fighting for his life. Chris stormed in the dayroom, ran to JC, and pulled him away from the other juveniles.

"Yeah, that's right! We told you we was gonna get that ya. Who mama you wanna talk about now?" one kid shouted.

Then another one put in his two cents, stating, "That's for all my homegirls and fam you was messin' wit, hoe. Don't worry. It's more where that came from."

The threats and boasting continued as Chris whisked JC into C hall away from the mini riot that had exploded in the dayroom. JC was bloody and bruised, again. This was the third and definitely most severe beating

JC had taken in less than a month. Chris called over the radio and told the control room monitor to call 911. He didn't want to leave JC, but he knew he had to get back to the dayroom to help his fellow DOs.

The chaos had ceased. Everyone was ordered back to their rooms, and everyone complied. The facility was on lockdown. After getting all the kids into their rooms, the DOs met in the control room. Chris slung open the door to the control room and was the first to break the awkward silence. "What was that? What happened?"

Mike spoke up first. "It was a freakin' ambush. By the time we got one kid off JC, two others came to take his place. They whupped that boy bad. We just didn't have enough people to save him."

"Who started it?" Chris inquired.

"I don't know. It all happened so fast."

"Who was the control room monitor?" Chris asked.

All the DOs answered in unison: "Kyle" (who was still in the bathroom at this very moment).

"Well, where is he?" said Chris.

Seconds later, the bathroom door of the control room opened, and out stepped Kyle like a frightened baby. "So you tellin' me that while all this happened, you ran in the bathroom?"

Kyle kept his head hung in shame. "I was scared, all right? I didn't know what else to do, so I ran."

Kayla, the smart butt of the group, laughed and stated, "Oh, you so fired."

Chris scanned the room and recognized another DO's absence. "And wait a minute, where is Holley?"

There was no answer to this question. She had not been seen since the first set of restraints had started. Holley was notorious for starting trouble and running from the aftermath. The major problem at hand was the fact that the camera system was not up and running yet, so there was no way to truly determine who started the uproar and who all was involved.

Johnny had just returned from getting supplies for the facility from downtown. As he walked in to see the faces of his exhausted and infuriated DOs, he quickly threw out there. "I don't even want to know right now." This was a one heck of a mess. Not to mention JC had not yet received the medical attention that was needed for him.

The ambulance finally showed up, and JC was taken to the clinic. Chris escorted him to the clinic, but not one word was shared between them throughout the entire visit. The hours of paperwork were diligently waiting for Chris at his return. None of the stories matched. It was almost as if someone had started a game of telephone. Everyone painted their own conclusion. Chris could not find a home to rest his anger. He did not know whether to be upset with Holley for her ignorant and spiteful actions, with the superintendant for making such a prideful judgment in the handling of JC, or the ever-so-reliable ignorance of an angry teenager.

Seven hours of paperwork later, the incident had been "adequately" reported. At 5:00 a.m., Chris still followed through faithfully with his ritual of praying for the kids. He prayed for A hall, then B hall, and then walked into C hall to check on JC. There was no major damage done to JC, but his pain didn't know that. I'm not sure there was a place on his body that didn't make contact with a foot or a fist.

He opened JC's door and walked in. JC was sitting on top of his desk with his head in his hands. He had no words for JC, only a silent prayer. As Chris was walking out, JC called his name.

"Yes, son?" Chris replied.

"Do you think I can still get in your class?"

Chris took it as a joke at first. "Why on earth would you want to take my class now?"

JC stood up and walked to Chris and looked at him face-to-face. "Every person in that room attacked me, but none of them attacked me for anything I had done to them. Everybody was mad behind a sister or a friend or a girlfriend, sadly even a mom. Chris, I don't know how to treat a woman right. I don't even know how to treat my own mama right. I think yesterday may have been the first time in my life she had referred to me as her baby and said I love you without question in her voice. I see what she was talkin about now. I see that I'm doing to others what men did to her. I can't do it no more. The bloodshed stops here. I've done so much, Chris. So much. But I promise I want to make it right. Will you teach me, Chris?"

Chris was blown away. "Yes, son. I'll teach you."

Earlier that day, Tomika had fallen to her knees and began to pray. "Dear God, I know you don't hear from me too often, and I'm sorry. I know that you are real now. I just want to say thank you for sending me Erin. I have wondered for so long if you were real, but Erin has shown me that you are really up there and you do love me. So, God, I'm trying to give my life to you. And I ask you for one thing. Oh God, I pray that you save my son. Humble him and let him know that you are there. I know that you will protect him, God. Well, I guess that is it. Thank you, sir. I mean God! Amen."

Ain't it amazing how God can work? Now, of course, it seemed like a terrible thing for JC to be beat like he was. But without that experience, he may have never seen the error of his ways. We also had the chance to see what happens when you let your pride get the best of you. And we definitely can't forget the oh-so-important lesson of unity. This chapter was just filled with life lessons. While you are reading this book, please don't get so lost in entertainment and drama that you miss out on the message. These are real-life problems. We need more young men as well as old men stepping up to the plate to raise these young men in our world today.

Chapter 8

Everything That Glitters Ain't Gold

I know some of my messages may be getting a little redundant, but treat it as if I'm a teacher getting you ready for a test. When a teacher prepares his students for a test, he often repeats the most important information. So once again, this is a newsflash to my Christians, saints, preachers, pastors, ministers, evangelists, or whatever other title you would like to fall under. We have developed a bad habit of being a prime example of a hypocrite. We condemn the world for actions that we do daily. We are quick to let someone know that what is done in the dark will come to the light as if we are exempted from that rule. Every day we are making the God we claim we serve appear more and more fake. Let's get it together and let's be the light unto the world that God has called us to be. 'Cause if we do that, the light just might show us just how far we need to come. Just remember, the only difference between a sinner and someone that's saved is the saved person knows to ask for forgiveness and repent.

Erin and Tomika had become inseparable. From work to home, they spent all their time together. Tomika was beginning to resemble the little girl that was so full of light in high school. It was a Saturday night, and the two were at Erin's house playing cards and watching movies. Erin had been waiting for the chance to invite her new friend to church, and she felt this was it. "Hey, Tomika, will you go to church with me tomorrow?"

Tomika looked up with a hesitant look. "Why do you want me to go to church?"

"Well, that is the next step in learning about God. It's more than just praying and reading the Bible. The Word tells us not to fail to fellowship with one another. It's how we learn to walk this walk with Christ. I have started going to this church not too far from work. The preaching and teaching has been great, and the women of the church have been so sweet and loving to me. Oh, girl, please come visit with me tomorrow."

Tomika was so scared. Just the word *church* sent chills down her spine. "Well, Erin, to tell the truth, I have had some pretty bad experiences with church people. I was talking to this guy in college and he was a preacher. What he didn't tell me was he was married. When his wife found out that we had slept together, her and all her church friends started calling me and threatening me. They started all these rumors about me that I was a homewrecker and I was a slut and how I was gonna burn in hell for what I was doing. And to make matters worse, he wasn't the only man at that church I had been with and they was all married. I don't like church people. They just a bunch of hypocrites. I can't tell you how many times I've watched so-called church people claim how much they love God and speak the Word and turn right around and talk about people like they are dogs. They are some truly evil people."

Erin walked over to her and placed her hand on her shoulder. "Girl, you ain't telling me nothing that I don't already know."

That was the last thing Tomika expected to hear from someone trying to convince her to go to church. "I had the same problem. I'm not a perfect person, but I'm trying. But some of the churches that I have been to have made me sick to the stomach. I have had married pastors try to sleep with me. And that ain't even the worst part. One of them tried to read some of the Old Testament to me and say that he was a king and God said that he was allowed to have concubines so it was all right. So I understand completely. But answer me this. How many dirtbag mechanics are out there that don't fix nothing and will completely take advantage of you?"

Tomika shook her head.

"Girl, I can name five off the top of my head."

Tomika replied with a laugh.

"Okay would you even go as far to say there are many more bad mechanics than the good ones?"

Tomika thought for a second. "I would say out of every ten mechanics, nine of them ain't worth the grease they work in."

Erin smiled. "So, Tomika, knowing that there are that many bad mechanics, if your car is broke, does that mean you aren't gonna take your car to get fixed?"

Tomika responded quickly, "Girl, please. You just have to take your chances and try and find a good one. And when you find the good one, you hold on to him."

Erin jumped up and said, "That's right, girl, but it's the same thing with church. You can't just give up on all them 'cause there are some good ones out there. You just have to take your chances, and when you find a good one, you hold on to it."

Tomika was at a loss for words. She was still hesitant about it, but she agreed to go to church with Erin. "But, girl, I ain't got nothing to wear. I can't go up in God's house lookin' all tore up."

Erin just looked at her and shook her head. "Tomika, don't even try it 'cause we wear the same size and I got more clothes than I know what to do with, so now what."

Tomika folded her arms. "You get on my nerves. You always got an answer for something. But I ain't gonna lie, that mechanic analogy was fly. But you still get on my nerves."

Erin looked back with a grin. "That was a tight lil analogy. I know, gurl. I know," she stated in a playful tone.

The next morning, the young ladies woke up and got ready for church. Tomika was still nervous but was going to keep her word. As they drove to the church, Tomika kept hearing all the hurtful things the women and members had said to her in the past. A few tears fell as she rode in silence. When they pulled up to the church, Tomika felt like a little girl going to her first day of school. She sat in the car, simply staring at the cross on top of the building.

Erin walked around to her door and tapped on the glass. "Are you all right, Tomika? If you really aren't ready, then let me know and we can wait."

Tomika rejected Erin's offer. "No, no. I'm ready. I was just daydreaming."

Tomika was determined to face her fears. The two ladies walked up to the doors as the music and singing flooded out the sanctuary. Tomika was overwhelmed by a feeling she couldn't relate to. The ushers greeted them with hugs and smiles. They were then shown to their seats. It was youth Sunday, so the children were in charge of the service. Two young girls were leading praise-and-worship service. They were singing with a pure praise that this world rarely sees. The song was called "Oh How I Love Jesus." Tomika was in utter awe. She could only hold her hand to her heart and close her eyes as the song ministered to her spirit. She felt a peace that was exponentially more significant than anything she had ever felt. After praise and worship was finished, one of the cutest little boys walked to the front of the church and gave the welcome. The program then began.

Several youth began their scripture readings, praise dances, exhortations, and poem readings. Tomika was filled with joy as she watched the young children offer their gifts to God. It was so beautiful how the scriptures flowed from the babe's lips. So heartwarming watching the young girls tug on the strings of God's heart with their dancing. But nothing affected Tomika like the poem that was rendered by a young girl. This sweet teenage princess walked to the microphone and began to let her soul speak to the congregation. "Hello, saints. My name is May, and I will be reading a poem today called 'Jesus, Are You Really There.'" She took a deep breath, closed her eyes, and began.

"Jesus, do you hear me? I'm in so much pain. At times I search for sunshine, but all I find is rain. I must ask, do you love me? 'Cause I must say I don't know. 'Cause if you love me, why do you let them hurt me so. Even they say they love me, then they threw my innocents to the dirt. Jesus, why, oh why, is it that if you love me, you just let my heart hurt? Do you hear me when I cry? Do you care if I die? Why is it that when they say they didn't do it, they get away with their lie. There is so much that happens in the world today—wars, disease, and death. Why don't you make it go away? Men that lie, steal, cheat on their wives, and that is far from it. After all their deeds are done, they stand behind your pulpit. They proclaim your name, sing of your praise, and declare your goodness and love, but every other action detest your presence from up above. Oh God, I'm mad at you, and if you punish me, I don't care. I have made up my mind, Jesus, you are not really there. But before I could finish my thought, you wrapped me in your arms and you whispered, 'May, I am here.' My heart skipped a beat. I couldn't move my feet. I was completely lost in my fear. you showed me your presence as you began to ease my pain. My heart was filled with joy, and I could only call your name. For your presence was so divine, and of this truth I couldn't deny. For at this moment all my fears were calmed, and in you my heart could rely. So yes, I stand here before you today and proclaim that to his love no pain can compare. And that no matter what the devil tells me, I believe—no, I'm sure. No, I know, my brothers and sisters in Christ, that yes, Jesus is really there."

There was not a dry eye in the sanctuary. The young girl's words pierced the hearts of so many people that the pastor skipped his message he had planned to preach and began altar call. Women, men, and children alike began to praise God and lift their hands in worship. The choir began to sing as the pastor and ministers began to pray for the people that fled to the altar. God's spirit was so strong in the house that first-time visitors and nonbelievers began to crowd the aisles to give their lives to God and be saved.

Tomika was still sitting in her seat, waving her hand and crying. "Jesus. Jesus, I need you. For the longest time, I didn't know if you were there, but now I believe. Oh God, I believe. God, I want to be born again." Right as she whispered those words from her heart, a minister came and grabbed her by her hand. Tomika thought to herself, *God? Is that you?*

The minister guided her from her seat and said, "Dear woman, God told me to come and pray with you. He said that you have already done the hard part by welcoming him in your life."

Tomika fell to her knees as she cried even harder than before because of the confirmation that God gave her through the minister. The minister kneeled down to her and whispered in her ear, "All you have to do now is confess with your mouth because you already believe in your heart that Jesus Christ died for your sins and he rose on the third day with all power in his hands."

Tomika whispered the words the minister had spoken, and after the last word departed from her mouth, she was overcome by a supernatural force. Tomika was filled with the Holy Spirit. As she lay on the ground, she was oblivious to every other person present in the church. It was simply her and God. Her spirit began to fellowship with him, and she was truly at peace. One hour later she was picked up by two of the ushers that placed her back in her seat.

The pastor stood before the church and began to speak. "Saints of God, in all my years of ministry, I have never seen the Spirit of God move like this. May, where are you? Come here, baby."

The young girl walked to her pastor still lifting her hands in worship.

"This young lady was truly used by God to lift some strongholds that the enemy has had over so many of us. Even I myself can remember when I questioned if God was really there. So I want to thank you, young woman of God, for blessing our souls with the gift that God gave you."

At that moment Tomika burst from her seat and ran to the altar and fell at the young girl's feet. She took May by her hands and said, "Thank you, May. I want to thank you for bringing me to God. Thank you so much."

The pastor was so overwhelmed by what God showed him had happen in Tomika's heart that he was moved to ask her to testify. As Tomika began to hug the young teen, the pastor placed his hand on Tomika's shoulder and said, "Ma'am, will you tell the people what God has done for you today?"

Tomika rose up with a boldness she had never known. The pastor handed her the microphone, and she turned to the crowd. "I never knew my father. I have had a feeling of emptiness since the day my mother told me the truth about him. And that was that he didn't want me and didn't love me. I tried to run from my pain for years by staying as busy as I could in school and sports. I tried to trick myself into believing that people loved me, but the truth was that they only loved what I could do. Finally

I thought that I found a man that loved me at my senior graduation party. He said all the right things and made all the right moves, and then he told me those three little words that I had been longing to hear for eighteen years of my life. And when he said he loved me, I gave myself to him. But he didn't love me, and it hurt me so bad that he lied. And the Devil told me that no man would ever love me. So I wanted to prove him wrong. So I went through a period of my life where I gave myself to any man that told me he loved me because it calmed my fear of never being loved. After being used and abused by man after man, I lost myself. Then a few years later I got pregnant and had a son. And while I was pregnant, I made up in my mind that I was going to hate all man for what was done to me. I even told God to give me a daughter and spare me the pain of having to hate my son. But he gave me a son, so I started to hate God too. I spent all of my son's life working and providing for him, but I never raised him. I disciplined him and made sure he had food, clothes, and shelter, but I never truly gave him love. I was too busy making him pay for every other man that ever hurt me. Then on his birthday, he said something to me that reminded me of the first man that hurt me, so I beat on him and I threw him out of the house. The last thing he said to me before he walked out the house was 'You didn't even tell me happy birthday, Mom.' Once he walked out that door, I sat in my house and the devil spoke to me like never before. He told me that no one would care if I died and that I should just kill myself. So I slashed my wrist and took over thirty-seven pills. I remember telling myself as I lost consciousness that no one would care. No one would miss me. And then I woke up in the hospital with one of my coworkers asleep in the chair next to me. I was so ugly to her and I told her to leave. But instead of giving up on me, she prayed for me. That was the first time in years I had felt any peace at all. After that she never left my side. She took off work and stayed with me while I was in the hospital, and I couldn't understand it. Why was this woman still here after I was ugly to her and made her leave, and she said because she loved me. And that scared me more than I can express. But she kept bringing me closer and closer to God. Even when I told her about my past, she didn't judge me. She kept loving me and praying for me and teaching me the Word, and I tell you that she is a true woman of God. And I love you for letting God use you to save my life, Erin. Then she asked me to come to church and I started telling her about how churches had done me just like this little girl read in her poem. And she told me that churches are like mechanics. There are plenty of bad ones, but you have to search until you find a God one and hold on to it."

The church agreed with hand claps and amens. Once the applause ceased, she continued. "Well, I must be honest. I was so scared to come here today and find the same treatment I found in other churches, but from the second I made it to the steps, I had a warm feeling. The program was so beautiful, and I enjoyed myself so much. But when this baby came up and read this poem, I felt like she had opened my chest and began to read from the hidden parts of my heart. And when she finished, for the first time in my life, God showed himself to me in a way that I couldn't deny. It was like fire in my body. I told God that I want to be born again. And as soon as I said that, a minister came and told me how to be saved. And as soon as I confessed it with my mouth, I felt the Holy Spirit come into my soul. I had read about the Holy Spirit, but there is no way to explain it. For however long I was on that floor, it was only me and God. I am free! I am free! I know Jesus is there! I know he is! And I stand to tell the Devil today that a man does love me, and his name is Jesus."

The church began to worship and praise God all over again for the birth of a new sister in Christ. After service and all the hugs Tomika could stand, she was approached by the pastor. "Young lady, I want to thank you for coming and blessing us with your testimony, and I want you to know that you are welcome here any time."

Tomika smiled. "Yes sir, Pastor. I do feel welcome and will be back."

Tomika and Erin walked to the car and just sat there. They were too tired to even drive home, so they just sat and fell asleep in the car. Tomika looked over at Erin and said, "Girl, if I'm gonna come back here, I need to get in shape."

Erin laughed and replied, "You and me both, girl. I ain't never hugged that many people in my life. My arms feel like they about to fall off."

Earlier that morning, at the detention center, as JC lay in his bed, he prayed to God. "Mr. God, sir. I was reading in your Word that you can make people whole and that you can deliver them. Well, my mom is hurting from something that she never told me, but I know it's from her past. Well, I guess I was kinda wondering if you would deliver her from whatever it is. I love my mom so much, but I'm just now learning what love is. So can you help us to learn to love each other please? Well, uh, thank you, Mr. God, sir. Amen. Oh yeah, and tell your son, Jesus, I said hi too. Thank you."

I don't even know if I should even give a closing thought on this chapter. It is truly a shame that "the church" seems no different and, at times, is even worse than the world. We may never know how many people we have turned away from God by our actions. Oh, the courage of that young girl to step out and be real with God. How many of us have felt the exact same way but were terrified to admit it, not to even consider expressing it. When we let these things become our testimonies, we give so many people hope.

Tomika has made her way to Jesus. I get chills from this chapter just knowing how good and real my Jesus is. But tears follow after the thought because I see how often we, as children of God, make him seem like a fairy tale. Tomika's prayer for her son was answered, and now JC's prayer for his mom has been answered. Contrary to what the Devil may want you to believe, God still answers prayers.

Chapter 9

Where Did You Learn That?

When a little child says something that he is not supposed to say, the first question that is asked is, "Who taught you that?" Many negative behaviors are adapted from the parents. Some are adapted from siblings. Others are picked up from peers or influences. Now let's look at the order I just gave. First we look at the parents. They are the constant example for the children. So this does away with the oh-so-famous saying. "Do as I say and not as I do." Your child learns from watching you. Following that, we have siblings. I'm sure some of you were that little brother or sister that thought the world of your big brother or sister. Whatever they did you wanted to do as well. Next we have peers. Now if you are reading this book, then that means you went to school and you know all too well about the power of peer pressure. We want to fit in or "be cool," so we do things to gain acceptance, often overriding whether these things are right or wrong. Then we have influences. These are the actors, athletes, and artists that we try to mirror our life after. Now let me ask you a question. Which one of these things do you think lead the majority of our children in this generation?

The day had finally come. The smoke had finally cleared with the riot, and it was time for Chris to get started with the class. The children were split into three groups of five in order to have a more personal touch on the class. Each group was given one hour for their class time. Group 1 consisted of Andrew, Sean, Christian, Isaiah, and Mouse. The class was taught in one of the school classrooms. As the young men walked in, they looked a little worried. They were not sure what they had gotten themselves into. The five young men took their seats and awkwardly stared at each other.

Chris stood up with a huge smile on his face and ecstatically said, "Welcome to From Boys to Gentleman. I will be your teacher in this class, and I'm so happy to have you bright young men here with me today. This class is on a voluntary basis only. You don't have to take this class if you don't want to. Let me give you a brief introduction of the class, and then you will able to decide if you want to make the commitment to this course. The purpose of this class is to learn to carry yourself as respectful young men. The mission statement is I will learn to treat woman like I would want my mother, sister, future wife and daughter to be treated. We will have open discussion, written work, and presentations in this class. There are two rules in this class. You will respect others and their opinions at all times no matter what is said, and you will keep an open mind. Any disciplinary problems in this class will result in forty-eight-hour confinement and revoking of all visitation privileges. Now, does anyone want to leave this class at this time?"

The kids gave a unanimous no.

Chris then placed a contract and pencil on each desk. "Well, now I want to get on a personal level with you boys. I am doing this class because I love ya'll. This is your class. You can get as little or as much as you put into it. Now don't play with me on this, fellas. I'm giving my all in this. Can I expect the same from ya'll?"

Isaiah stood up and was the first to say, "I'm wit you, Chris. You got my word, homie. I mean, sir." The other four did the same and signed the papers.

"That's my boys. Well, let's get started. Today is open discussion. I throw out a topic and I want each of you to tell me how you feel about it. Now I'm gonna allow ya'll to speak freely as long as it don't get out of hand. But before we do that, I want each of you to stand up, give your name, and tell me why you are here, Andrew, you start."

The young man stood up and walked to the front. "My name is Andrew Garcia, a.k.a. Baby A. I'm fourteen years old, and I'm in here for whupping some dudes that was tryin' to disrespect my set."

"Thank you, Andrew. Christian, you are next."

"Well, my name is Christian Smith, aka Lil C. I'm thirteen years old. I'm in here 'cause I got caught with some dope and for skipping school."

Next was Sean. "My name is Sean Wright, and I ain't got no aka. I'm just Sean."

Chris smiled.

"Uhhhhh, I'm fifteen years old, and I'm in here 'cause I ain't no snitch, you feel me?"

Isaiah followed. "My name is Isaiah Parker. I'm seventeen, and I'm in here because I beat up this fool that was disrespectin' my moms and my sister. He was trying to treat my sister like a lil hoe, and then when my mom asked him to leave, he called her *b*. So I whopped that tail."

Last but not the least was Mouse. Chris stood up and stopped the young man. "Mouse, what is your real name 'cause I don't even know."

The kids laughed but were also intrigued because they didn't know either.

"Well, my name is Luke Moore. But that's my daddy's name, and I hate that punk, so I go by *Mouse* 'cause I'm small, quick, and cute."

Chris laughed. "Now I like that. The small, quick, and cute is clever. That's what you be tellin' them young ladies, ain't it?"

Mouse poked out his chest and popped his collar and replied, "And you know this, man. But anyways, I'm fifteen and I'm in here because I was sellin' that work to feed my little sister and brother."

"Okay, fellas, let's get started with the discussion."

Mouse objected. "Hold up, Mr. Chris. You didn't tell us about you and why you here."

"Well, okay, that's fair. My name is Christopher Shayne Daughtery. I'm twenty-three, and I'm in here 'cause I love to help people and because water, lights, gas, and food ain't free."

The kids laughed.

"Now that my intro is over, let's get down to biz. The first thing I want to know is, who is your male hero? Who is that person that you just look up to in life?"

The room was silent as the young men racked their brains trying to come up with the perfect answer. Finally Sean spoke up, "My hero is Lil Wayne."

Isaiah snapped his fingers and replied, "Awww, man, you took mine. That was who I was gonna say."

Sean continued explaining, "He got so much money and he get all the hoes."

Chris inquired to the young man's selection. "Do you have anybody that is in your family or that is in your life that you look up to?"

"Naw, ain't really no men in my family. But I look up to my OG 'cause he a boss and he make stuff happen. I want that kind of power."

Christian followed with his hero. "My hero is Jay-Z. He rich, he know Lebron James, and he got Beyoncé! You can't go wrong with that."

Andrew was next. "My Hero is T. I. I want to be like him so I can tell them hoes you can have whatever you like. You feel me?"

Once again Mouse was the only one left. Chris attempted to encourage him to speak. "What about you, Mouse? Who is your hero?"

The young man thought about it as he stared up to the ceiling with his head cocked to the side. It was clear that Mouse was searching for an answer that would be accepted by the other boys. He was afraid of the rejection of his peers. He had an image to uphold. Finally, he answered. "My hero is Lil Bow Wow. He a lil dude too, but he be getting that baddest chicks. Just like Ciara. She was like a foot taller than him, but he still had her walking down the red carpets and writing songs about him. That's a true player right there."

His choice got the approval of all his peers as they agreed and gave him high fives and dap. "Okay, let's go to our next topic. I want ya'll to tell me your opinions on females."

Mouse was the first to chime in on this one. "Oh, I got this one, Chris. A female is a prize. They are like money. You can never have enough of them. But only the flyest guys get the flyest girls."

"Oh, okay. Well, can you elaborate for me. What do you mean get them?"

"Well, it can mean whatever. You got different types of girls. Some girls can be ya main. The chick that come before everybody else. Then you got ya side chicks. They cool to kick it with, but you don't ever get too serious with them. Then you got ya hoes. Them the girls you just hit then you send them on they way."

Chris had a hard time holding his opinions back, but it wasn't time for his two cents to be put in. So he just inquired a little deeper into what the young men were saying. "Okay, so how do you tell the difference between a girl that is supposed to be a main and a girl you just consider a side chick or a hoe?"

Sean took the lead for this one. "It's easy. When you find a good chick that got some class and ain't a hood rat, you can make her ya main. When a girl act like a hoe, that's what I treat her like."

Isaiah joined in with his thoughts. "Yeah, he right. If a girl just letting you hit, then why would I turn it down? Then you got them little weak girls that ain't really hoes but they like you so much that they will do anything to be with you. So if you that stupid, then I'm gonna take advantage."

Chris was amazed by the statements the young men were making. "So does everyone agree with this?"

They all agreed. They shared the same views when it came to the young ladies.

"Well, okay, we have time for one more topic. I want each of you to tell me about your relationship with your father."

The atmosphere of the room transformed dramatically. There was a surge of anger and pain that was radiating off the young boys without a word being spoken. "Andrew ... Sean ... Christian ... Isaiah ... Mouse? Anybody?"

Nobody had a word to say. Sean finally broke the silence. "I ain't got no father. I got a sperm donor. My daddy left me and my mom when I was ten. I'm glad he left too. He used to beat on my mom and sisters. I remember one time he was beating on my mom and I ran in to try and stop him. He pushed me on the ground and he looked me in my eyes, and he told me that when my hoe don't listen, I need to put her in a hoe's place. He just kept slappin' her, and my mom just kept crying and asking him to stop. When he was done, he went and sat in the kitchen. I went up to him and I asked him why he was hitting my mommy. He told me that his daddy taught him to never let a woman disrespect him, and when she don't listen, you whup her butt. He said that a woman is like a child. If you don't whup them, then they will run all over you. So I hate that bastard for hitting my mom."

Chris was disturbed by the young man's story. "I'm so sorry to hear that, Sean. Did he ever teach you anything else?"

"Oh yeah, he taught me a lot. He taught me how to play ball. He taught me how to ride my bike, and he taught me how to get girls. He taught me all about females and the game. But none of that mattered once he started hitting my mom."

"I see," Chris replied. "I'm truly sorry to hear that."

Out of the five, only Sean and Isaiah even knew who their father was. Isaiah did not want to speak about his father. The rest just talked about their OG or a uncle or big brother. These were the men that picked up the slack of where a father left his son. Isaiah asked, "What about you, Chris. You didn't give us your answers. We want to know what you got to say since you got us talking like we on Oprah."

Chris stood in front of the young men and gave his answers. "My hero is my grandfather. Him and grandmother raised me from birth. He is one of the main reasons that I'm the man that I am today. To me a female is not a prize, but a gift. Females are the mothers, sisters, daughters, and friends. Needless to say, my relationship with my father was nonexistent. I have never known my biological father, but God gave me my grandfather."

Mouse raised his hand and asked, "Don't it make you mad that your dad left you?"

Chris took a deep breath and replied, "Yes, Mouse. It made me so mad. I spent much of my young life asking why my dad didn't want me. Why was I such trash to him? It was a shame that it took me so long to truly see what I had with my grandpa. Let me tell you a quick story. Back in elementary, we had a field day. It was kind of a father-son day. The main event of the day was the father-son relay. Now at this time, my grandpa was about sixty-five years old. But let me tell you, my grandpa was fast. I could not really beat him in running until I was twelve. And when I did beat him, it was by steps. Well, all the other kids had their fathers and they were all young and in Nike shorts and shoes, stretching and getting ready for the race. My grandpa showed up in his cowboy boots, jeans, and an old button-up shirt. He used to walk around looking like a black John Wayne. But anyways, it was time for the race. All the other kids started laughing at me and making jokes about my grandpa racing. They was asking me if he needed a wheelchair or if they need to have 911 on speed dial for after the race. I got mad, and then I thought, my grandpa is one of the fastest people I ever met. So I was up first. I ran as hard as I could to make sure he had a good lead. I got the baton back to him and told him to go. He waited till the other kids got back and let the other dads take off. I was yelling at the top of my lungs, 'Go, Papa. Hurry up.' He finally took off. Man, my papa dusted all of them young daddies. He crossed the finish line and came to me and picked me up for a victory jog. All the other kids were mad at their dads for losing to the old man. You know I had to get my trash talk in. I walked up to them and asked them, 'Who needs the wheelchair now?' It was that day that helped me realize just what a blessing I had in my grandpa."

All five of the young men seemed to be fighting tears. Chris had really struck a soft spot on these kids.

"Well, fellas, time is up. Thanks for your time. Here is your homework. I want all of you to think of your three top songs and music videos. Then I want you to think about the women you love most in your life."

"All right, Chris, we got you. See ya tomorrow."

The two following classes turned out with almost the exact same results. All the young men were so misguided on what life was about. After those classes, Chris had one more student. JC was brought into the classroom. Chris took a different approach than he did with the other kids because he knew that there were not many females, if any, that he could use to teach JC what he was trying to teach him. "JC, I want you to tell me about your life. I really want to know where you are coming from."

The question caught JC off guard. No one had ever asked him anything like this before. "What do you want to know?" JC replied.

"Son, I want to know whatever you want to tell."

JC began to cry. "What do you want from me, man. You have to want something. You always checking on me and praying with me and trying to teach me stuff. Now you coming at me like you care how I feel. I want to believe you, but it's hard. People been using me all my life. Everybody, from coaches, teachers, hoes, everybody. What do you want from me! I don't like this feeling! What is this!"

Chris walked over to the young man. "Look at me, JC. I know it's hard to trust people. There are not many that I trust. I need you to look me in my eyes when I speak to you."

JC looked up at Chris as the tears continued to flow.

"I am going to do whatever it takes for you to trust me. And you're right, I do want something from you."

JC began to get mad and tried to turn cold. "I knew you wanted something. You just like everybody else. How could I be so dang stupid—"

Before the young man could finish his transformation back into his cold and careless state, Chris interrupted him. "You know what I want from you? I want you to try and let me teach you how to be loved and to love."

Once again JC lost all composure and buried his face in Chris's chest. Like before, it seemed that God was answering his prayer. After a few minutes to get himself together, JC began to tell Chris all about his life. Everything, from when he first started playing ball to how he got to JDC.

"Look, JC, I'm not going to play any games with you. I'm gonna ask you straight up, and I expect an honest answer. Do you want to change and learn how to become a gentleman?"

JC replied quickly. "Hell yeah, I wanna—I mean, yes, sir, I really do."

Chris smiled. "Well, let's get started. First of all, I need you to know that you are a slut. But I understand why you are like that. You have to learn to treat women like you want someone to treat your mom or future daughter."

JC began to think about Cherish. "There was this one girl. She was different. We actually talked. She made me chase her. I really started liking her. At first I was just trying to hit it, but as I spent time with her, then I really wasn't even thinkin' about sex. Then one night she said something that reminded me of what one of my old coaches had told me. Then I started tripping. I thought that she was out to get me, but now I think—naw, I know now that she really cared about me. I wish I could take it back. I know I hurt her so bad."

"Well, what was her name?"

JC spoke softly. "Cherish Ward."

Chris's eyes shoot wide open. "Cherish Ward?" Chris had to catch himself. The young lady that JC was talking about was his mentor and father figure JW's daughter. He quickly changed the subject. "So do you know why it's so important to change how you treat women? Well, I'll tell you. The reason why there are so many children without fathers is because it takes a man to teach a boy how to be a man. You can only teach someone what you know. A man that only knows the drums can't teach someone else how to play the piano. The same way a man that only knows how to be a boy can't teach you how to truly be a man."

JC was a little lost. "Wait a minute, Chris. What does the drums have to do with being a man?"

Chris laughed. "It's an analogy. Let me see if I can put it in a way that you will understand better. Okay, if you were having a problem with your shot, would you go to a rebounding coach?"

"No. Why would I go to a rebounding coach for shooting? I'm going to go to a shooting coach."

Chris shouted with excitement, "Exactly! If you want to be a man, why would you go to someone that only knows how to be a boy?" It was as if Chris actually saw a light bulb go off on top of JC's head. Chris had found his avenue to teach the young man. Basketball!

"Oh, I get it. That really makes sense. I never thought about it like that. Okay, so let me ask you a question. You say that you are supposed to treat a woman like you want your mama to be treated, right? So what about them h—females that just act like that word I was about to say? A lot of females don't respect themselves, so why should I respect them?"

Chris thought for a second. "Okay, well, let's play like you are a coach for a second. You have a player that is fast, strong, can jump out of the gym, has a shot and super quick feet. But he was never taught to play defense. Worse than that, all his other coaches told him that he shouldn't worry about D 'cause scoring points is all that matters. You know how important it is to play defense in order to win. So do you tell him that he sucks and leave him on the bench?"

JC replied quickly, "Hell no. You teach that boy how to play defense. How is he gonna play good D if no one teaches him? Especially if no one tells him that he needs to. That ain't fair to just put him on the bench for something he don't know and no one has taught him. His past coaches should have been kicked in the head."

Chris stood in awe of the young man's knowledge of basketball. "Wow. I would love to have you as a coach. Well, just how you feel about that player you should feel the same way about that young girl. Is it her fault that no one ever taught her that she is a queen? Is it her fault that she doesn't know her worth?"

"Dang, C. I never thought about it like that. You're really making me feel like a dummy the way you making me answer my own questions."

Chris busted into laughter.

JC had another question for Chris. "Okay, Mr. Smart Guy. What about the females that have been told that they shouldn't act like that but they still do it?"

Once again Chris used JC's knowledge of basketball to answer his question. "If you are playing ball and someone fouls your teammate hard, do you foul the player hard?"

JC said, "Naw, you don't do that."

"Why not?" Chris inquired.

JC passionately explained his answer. "Just because somebody else don't know how to act don't mean you go and act stupid with them. That's how people get hurt and get their career cut short. That's just like when we had a tournament in Houston. This guy fouled me when I went up for a dunk. He took my legs out, and I fell on my back. Now if I had fouled him back, then I would have done nothing but teach my teammates that type of behavior is okay. Someone has to stand up and do the right thing in order for the game to continue. Wait a minute, you did it to me again. You are about to tell me that just because the girl don't respect herself that doesn't mean that I should treat her bad."

Chris stood and began to clap for the young man. "Bravo, bravo, good sir. You couldn't be more right. This is amazing. I don't have much to teach you. All I have to do is show you to apply how you view the game of basketball to life. Instead of just focusing on how you would want your mother or daughter to be treated, I want you to try and treat people like you would treat a teammate or the respect you show for an opponent. When someone says something to you out of line, pretend that you are at the free throw line and they are just trying to distract you from making the basket. When someone tries to get you off your game, you show the same focus that you have in a championship game. I think that once you get a closer relationship with your mother, then you will understand what I'm trying to teach these other young boys."

JC felt like a massive weight had been lifted off his shoulders. Someone had taken the time to teach him something that truly benefited him. There were no strings attached. He understood exactly what Chris was trying to teach him. More than that, he was ready to learn all the lessons he could. "I still don't understand you, Chris. Why do you even care what people do? I've watched you with these kids in here and how you treat them. Why do you care about us so much?"

Chris placed his hand on JC's shoulder. "First of all, I care because I love God. I see ya'll every day and I know that most of ya'll just haven't been taught. Just because you don't have your father doesn't mean that someone or something won't take his place. I know that if someone don't reach out to ya'll, then all that ya'll go through every day will just keep happening. The definition of insanity is repeating the same action, expecting a different result. For example, if I'm trying to drive to California from Texas but every time I leave my house I go east, how many times am I gonna make it to California? The only thing I can tell you is that I do care about ya'll. I love ya'll. But how will ya'll know I love ya'll if I don't show it?"

JC was even more lost than before. The more this man opened his mouth, the less he understood his motives. "Man, I still don't get it. I understand what you are saying, and it is 100 percent true, but don't nobody do what's right? But you know what? I can only make you one promise. I'm gonna try to trust you. I'm not gonna lie. You have done more for me than anybody else has just by talking to me and telling me what's real. I have spent so much of my life where people just told me what I wanted to hear instead of the truth. You got my word, Chris. I'm gonna do my best to change and become a gentleman."

The tables had now turned because for the first time, it was Chris trying to fight back the tears. "Thank you, JC. That means a lot to me."

Chris escorted JC back to his room. It was about time for Chris to make his rounds and pray for the kids, but he got a pleasant surprise this night. As he walked over to JC's bed to pray with him, JC interrupted him. "Hey, Chris, do you think I could pray for you tonight?"

Chris happily accepted the request to pray. JC closed his eyes and began. "Dear God, I just wanted to say thank you. It seems like the more I ask you for, the more you give me. I asked you to teach me and my mom how to love each other, and you sent this man to teach me. He has been so nice to me even when I was so terrible to him. I don't understand his kindness, but I'm thankful for it. God, I want you to be good to Chris 'cause he is so good to us. I think I love him, but I don't want to lie and say that 'cause I don't know if I can love yet. But I want to, God. God, I trust this guy even though I really don't want to. He really is the closest thing I ever had to a dad. I want to do this but I know I need help. I don't want to disappoint Chris and I don't want to disappoint you. So, God, please help us. I think I love you, God, and it scares me that I think you love me too. Well, I don't want to waste any more of this man's time, so I'm gonna stop. But I will talk to you some more when he leaves. Bye, God and Jesus. Amen."

Chris's attempt to hold back his tears had failed miserably. He had been overcome by the Spirit of God. Chris was overwhelmed with joy for the relationship the young man was gaining with God. All he could do was say thank you, Jesus, as he waved his hands in praise.

"Why are you crying, Chris?"

He hugged JC and said, "JC, you are on your way. You keep reaching for God and I promise he will reach back. I'm not crying because I'm sad. I'm crying because I'm so thankful for what God is doing in your life. I know you don't understand now, but I promise you will."

Chris then left and went to the bathroom to finish his praise and clean his face. He walked to the halls and he heard the young men talking about the class and the women that meant the most to them. Chris looked up and said, "God, you are really showing out. I'm thankful for you using me to do this."

Just as he left A hall from praying with the kids, JW turned Chris around and shook his hand. "Boy, I couldn't be more proud of you if you were my blood son. What you are doing with these kids is nothing short of amazing. I wish I had someone like you when I was coming up. There are a lot of young ladies that I hurt. You see, my dad taught me to go out and get as many females as I could and to never get attached. I was supposed to hold strong to my player ways. It wasn't until I had Cherish that my ways truly changed. But the Word is right when it says you will reap what you sow. Now some lil knucklehead done broke Cherish's heart. The thing that burns the most is that he told her the same thing I told this girl years ago back in high school. She asked him, why did he say that he loved her? And he told her that it sounded nice at the moment. I had to hold my baby girl knowing that I caused a girl the same pain that she was feeling that very second. I'd give anything to keep my baby from feeling that. And I'd give anything to be able to take back that night with Tomika. Don't you give up, Chris. I don't care what nobody tells you. You are doing the right thing and I'm behind you 100 percent. You hear me, son?"

"Yes, sir, I do. Thank you, Pops. Your support is needed and appreciated. If you don't mind me asking, who is Tomika?"

JW took a deep sigh. "Tomika Carter was a girl I met in high school. I had a crush on her since freshman year, but she was so wrapped up in sports and school that she didn't even know I was alive. Well, graduation night, we had a party and my boys caught me staring at her, and they started to clown me. They was calling me sprung and all that good stuff. Well, they were right. But I was young and dumb, so I had to protect my image and ego. They made me a bet that I couldn't have sex with her by the end of the night. I didn't want to take the bet, but the peer pressure got to me. Long story short, I pulled the dirtiest trick of them all and told her I loved her. The sad part was I thought that I really did love her. But we had sex that night, and when I got home, my boys was already trying to find out if I had won the bet. Once I told them I did, they spread the word to everybody.

"She showed up to my house the next day. I wanted to tell her the truth, but I didn't want to look like a punk in front of my boys. So I choose my image over my true feelings. She asked me why did I tell her I loved her, and like a smooth dummy, I told her because it sounded nice at the moment. My dad and boys thought that I was the coolest player ever, but I felt lower than dirt. I will never forget how she looked standing there as I walked off. I wish I could take back what I did to her. There are few things in my life that I regret more than that. That's why I'm so quiet in your class while you talking to the young men—'cause I was exactly where they are back in the day. I wish I was man enough to stand up and do the right thing. I was just taught all the wrong things. Now I just want to help young men know the truth. So if you don't mind, I would like to tell my story in your next class."

"Pops, I would be honored for you to do that."

It wasn't until Chris was driving home that he realized what he had learned today. Not only did he find out that JC was the "lil knucklehead" that had broke Cherish's heart, but the woman that Julian had hurt all those years back was JC's mom. "Oh crap, how is this gonna work? God, I'm really gonna need your help with this one."

Oh my. Where do I begin on this one? If you don't listen to anything else in this book, please hear these young men cry out for help. This is not just a story. This is what our young people are dealing with every day. How can we expect our young men to grow up to be men without a man to lead the way? I understand that the lack of a father is not always the case. I understand that some young boys turn out just fine without a father, but they have someone that teaches them what is right. But if we want to stop the lack of fathers in this world, we have to attack the problem at the root. Let's be real. We know where babies come from. So if we can teach a boy that a woman is more than a sexual plaything no matter who she is, then maybe that will start the corrective action needed for this problem.

I'm gonna talk to the fellas real quick. Brothers, have you ever tried to sleep with a girl and she wasn't having it? She thought too highly of herself to do that. Or she told you that she was waiting on marriage or love. Instead of getting mad at her, you should have stood up and gave her a round of applause. Because that is exactly what you would want your little girl to tell a boy trying to get between her legs. But more than likely, you called this young lady stuck-up or the single word for a female dog. Then you set your eyes on some girl that was what we like to call easy.

But what if you saw that girl that's easy in the same light as you would want someone to see your little girl or your sister? Look, my children of this generation, I understand that you are being taught that sex is the cool thing to do. Young ladies, you are learning every day that you have to be sexier to be anything. Young men, you are learning that without money and a large amount of women, you are nothing. But I refuse to stand here another day and not tell you the truth. You are kings and queens. Your worth will not be found in your body or your reproductive organs. It is in your hearts and spirits.

People that have grown up without the love of your father or your mother, I want you to take a minute and really think about the void that was left in your life by never having your father tell you he loved you. How you felt when you watched another child be taken somewhere by his father. How you felt at night when you asked God why he doesn't want you. For many of you that are in this situation, it was because your father was only looking for sex and was not mature or man enough to take care of a child because the truth is, he is still a child himself. So before you lie down with that boy or that girl, just stop and repeat something to yourself. "It's possible that I don't have my daddy or mommy because of the action that I'm about to do." Then I want you to think about those nights you spent longing for your father. If you can keep going after that, then I don't know what to tell you.

CHAPTER 10

What if She Meant Something to You?

It is so easy for us to emotionally detach ourselves when something happens to someone else. But what happens when it hits home? Someone that was hit by a drunk driver that you don't know is not much of a concern to you. But when it is your baby or loved one that is near death in a hospital bed, then you want to become a member of MADD (Mothers Against Drunk Driving). The same thing happens when it comes to the treatment of our women. A male can cheat and sleep with female after female, disregarding any emotional damage he may cause. But the second your sister or friend comes to you and tells you that some guy has broken her heart, you are ready to go give him the beating of a lifetime. Oh please, don't let it be your daughter that comes to you crying. At that point, you have typed the boys address into Google maps and have loaded your .22 special with hollow-point bullets. So here is my question. Why didn't you realize that all those girls that you ran through and/or abused were someone's sister, friend, or daughter?

The next day had come. Chris was up all night telling his girlfriend, Lisa, about the class. Lisa was so excited for him. She gave him so much support and insight. She told him of her bad experiences with boys. She also gave him some good ideas for the class. After the all-night session, Chris only had a couple of hours before work. When he got to work, he was greeted by his number one hater.

Holley wasted no time attempting to get under Chris's skin. "Chris, I don't know why you waste your time with those little thugs. I listen to the kids in their room talking about the class. They don't even take you serious. They were laughing at your grandpa story and talking about how you are so stupid. You should stop wasting everybody's time."

It was clear to him that Holley was upset with the success of the class after one day. "Oh, Holley, I didn't even see you there. How are you doing today? Is that a new hairstyle? Well, I'm running late. I will talk to you later. You have an amazing day."

Chris could feel the heat radiate from the angered woman's body as he walked by.

"Ha, ha, ha, you think you so dang funny, Chris, but don't worry, we will see who laughs last, you jerk."

Holley was right about one thing. The kids were talking about the class. They had not stopped talking about the class since yesterday and couldn't wait to get back to it. Before the class, it was visitation time. Even during the phone calls, the kids were talking about the Boys to Gentlemen class. They were boldly saying their mission statements and what they had talked about.

Chris walked into C hall and came to JC's door with a sad face. JC sprung off his bed and ran to the door. "What's up, Chris!" he shouted with excitement. He then saw Chris's face and his mood changed. "What's wrong, bro? Why you lookin' all down?"

Chris unlocked the door and asked JC to sit on his bed. "Look, JC, I'm sorry, but you can't have a phone call today."

"Aww, man, why not? I didn't get in no trouble. I want to tell my mom about the class. Come on, Chris. Is there anything you can do?"

Chris shook his head. "Sorry, JC, there is nothing I can do about your phone call."

JC was so upset. "But what did I do? Can you at least tell me why I can't have a phone call?"

Chris took a deep breath and exhaled. "Well, JC, you can't have a phone call because you're not allowed to have a phone call and a visit."

JC realized that Chris was playing a joke on him and almost hit his head on the ceiling jumping for joy. "You mean my mom is here?"

"Yes, sir, she is. Are you ready to go see her?"

JC gave no response; he simply ran to the door and waited for Chris to lead the way. As JC walked to the visitation room, his heart began to beat like a rabbit that drunk a gallon of red bull. As he entered the room, he ran to his mom and hugged her as tight as he could. "Oh, Momma, I have missed you so much."

Tomika was equally as excited to see her baby. "No, baby, I have missed you."

Neither of the two were used to this type of affection, period. But it felt more than amazing to both of them. They finally took their seats and began to talk. "Boy, you look so good. I see they feeding you good in here. How have you been?"

"Momma, good is an understatement. I don't even want to waste my time on the bad. So many good things have happened to me in here I don't know where to start."

Out of excitement of seeing each other, Tomika had forgotten to introduce Erin. "Oh, baby, I have someone I want you to meet. This is Erin. She saved my life, baby."

"Oh, so you are the lady that has been there for my mom. Do you mind if I hug you?"

"Do I mind? I was starting to get jealous after watching ya'll hug. Ha ha ha," Erin replied.

JC hugged Erin and whispered in her ear, "Thank you for saving my mom."

Erin whispered back, "It wasn't me, baby, it was God. I just let him use me to do it."

JC smiled. "Oh, Momma, I got to let you meet someone too. His name is Chris."

JC motioned for him to come in the room. Chris walked in and greeted Tomika and Erin. "How are ya'll doing, ladies? It's so good to meet ya'll."

Tomika shook Chris's hand and said, "I have heard so much about you, Mr. Chris."

JC began to tell his mom all about the class and everything that he was learning. Tomika and Erin were taken back with what JC told them. Both of the ladies began to cry. Chris quickly made his exit as the waterworks began. "Okay, ya'll enjoy the visit. Ya'll have about ten minutes left."

"Momma, Chris has introduced me to God. He prays with us every night. When we read the Bible and don't understand it, he explains it to us. I have been praying for you, Momma. I prayed that God would heal you from your past. I also prayed that we learn to love each other."

Tomika laughed. "That's funny, son, 'cause I have been praying for you too, dear. I prayed that you would become humble enough to let him into your life and that you would know that I love you. And it seems like he has answered both of those prayers. I'm so excited about our relationship, son. You keep being good in here and I will be coming to see you every day."

"Oh, Momma, thank you. I will look forward to it. Hey, before ya'll go, can I pray for us?"

Tomika was so shocked that she stood there speechless. She could only nod her head. The three of them joined hands as JC prayed. Chris watched from the outside and could only smile. After the prayer, he escorted Tomika and Erin out of the facility. But just as they were leaving, JW was bringing the next child out for visitation. He looked up and saw Tomika and immediately reverted back to the day he had left her standing in front of his house. It was as if he had seen a ghost. Tomika never noticed JW because she was too busy smiling at her son. JW still attempted to hide from her sight.

Once Chris had come back in and took JC to his room, JW called Chris back out to the visitation room. "What's up, Pops? You called me?"

"Yeah, you remember that girl I told you about yesterday? That woman that you took out just now was her. Did she come to see JC?"

Chris froze for a minute. He was unable to read JW or what he was thinking. Finally he answered, "Yeah, Pops. She was here to see JC. Look, Pops, I got to tell you something. I need you to be cool about it. I'm only telling you this 'cause I don't want you to find out from nobody else. The lil knucklehead that you were talking about yesterday is JC."

JW was confused. "What do you mean, Chris?"

Chris attempted to explain. "Look, Pops, don't you start trippin on me. JC is the boy Cherish was hurt by."

JW began to become enraged.

"Calm down, Pops. Now look, you said it yourself that you wish you could take back what you did. Well, JC feels the same way. Think about how you wished that you had someone to teach you the right thing. This is your chance."

JW began to calm down. "You're right, Chris. It is partly my fault that JC is even in the position he is in. Did she see me today?"

"Naw, Pops, I don't think she did. Are you still gonna be cool to help with the class today, or do you need some time to cool off?"

"Oh, no, I'm fine, son. As a matter of fact, I need you to trust me. I really want to talk to JC. I'm gonna tell him what I did to his mom and that I know about Cherish."

"Now, Pops, I'm trusting you. Don't make me regret this. You can't be choking kids and stuff."

"Ha-ha. Very funny, son."

It was time for day two of the class. The kids were super excited. The morning shift could not help but see how excited the kids were about the class. So they used that to their advantage. Any kid that got any article of discipline that day could not attend the class. One of the older DOs came up to Chris earlier that day and said, "Chris, I been working here for twenty-two years and I have never had a shift were nobody got in trouble.

I don't know what you doing to these kids, but they believe in you. Don't stop what you are doing, young man."

Chris was excited about the support that he was receiving from his coworkers, even though some of them were only happy because the kids were behaving, which made their jobs a breeze. But you know that there is always at least one person that has it in for you.

Well, it was class time and the first group came in. The young men walked in and sat down with their sheets of paper in front of them.

"Hello, fellas. Let's get started. Everyone stand up and raise your right hand."

Mouse was always the most outspoken. "Hey, Chris, what you got us raising our hands for? We bout to say the pledge of allegiance?"

Chris responded to the young jokester with a very serious demeanor. "No, Mouse, but we are going to say our mission statement. Now I'm all for having fun, but don't get disrespectful. I'm not saying your statement was disrespectful, but I can see how that type of outburst could become disrespectful on a different topic."

It was amazing how Chris was able to communicate with the young men. He always seemed to find away to get his message across in a way that the kids would receive it without feeling offended.

"Now please raise your right hand and read the mission statement off the board."

In unison, everyone read the statement. "I will learn to treat a woman like I would want my mother, my sister, or my future daughter to be treated."

The kids still did not truly understand the words they had just read, but oh were they in for a rude awakening. "Okay, who can tell me what I asked you to do for class last time?"

Sean took the lead. "You asked us to pick our favorite songs and videos. Then you wanted us to tell you who the most important women in our lives are."

Chris was impressed with his grasp of the assignment. "Okay, Sean, you start."

Sean walked up to the front of the room and began to read his sheet. "Okay, my top three songs are 'Shake Ya Tailfeather' by Nelly, ' Get in My Car' by 50 Cent, 'Girl Gimme Dat' by Webbie. My top three videos are, of course, *Tip Drill*, *Booty Poppin*, and *Make It Rain*. The most important women in my life are my mom, my lil sisters, and my aunts. They are so important to me."

Andrew followed with his list. "Okay, my top three songs are 'Whisper Song' by Ying Yang', 'In Luv With My Money' by Paul Wall, and 'Chamillionaire' and 'Lollipop' by Lil Wayne. I had to put a couple of throwbacks on there. My top three videos are *Tip Drill, Pull Over That A#$ Too Fat*, and I don't know if ya'll remember this one, but *Freek-a-Leek* by Petey Pablo 'cause that chick on that video was so bad that I would have gave her my life savings twice for just one night with her."

All the young men gave approval of his comments.

"Yeah, and my most important women are my mom and my sisters."

Isaiah was next. "I'm gonna change my songs 'cause Andrew took it back. My songs are 'Getting Some Head' by Shawna, 'What's Your Fantasy' by Ludacris, and 'I'm a Flirt' by R. Kelly. My videos are *Make It Rain* by Lil Wayne, *Play* by David Banner, and *Money Maker* by Ludacris. My women are my grandma, my aunts, and my daughter. I love my lil girl. I can't wait to get out of here and hold her."

Christian was excited about his turn. The young men were really enjoying the walk down memory lane. "Okay, my songs are '99 Problems' by Jay-Z, 'I'm in Love with a Stripper' by T-Pain, and 'I'm a P.I.M.P' by 50 Cent. My videos are *Right Thur* by Chingy—the uncut version—*Hot in Here* by Nelly, and *Tip Drill*. *Tip Drill* has to be the best video ever. The chick in the white had an booty that should be illegal to have. Anyways, my most important women are my mom, my sisters, and my girl!"

Last but definitely the craziest was Mouse. "Okay, I know I'm different, but I don't care 'cause this is just me. But my top songs are 'Grind on Me' by Pretty Ricky, 'Number One' by John Legend, and 'Bad Chick' by Webbie. My videos are *Tip Drill*, anything with Lil Kim in it, and *Thong Song*. Yes, I said *Thong Song*. As a matter of fact, I'm gonna put *Thong Song* and *Thong Song Remix*. There was so much booty in the videos I didn't even need a porno. And my important women are my mom, my sister, and my lil cousins."

Chris could only shake his head at the young man. "Okay, fellas, now we are going to do a little activity. I want you to take your papers and listen. All right, everybody, look at song number one on your paper. You are going to dedicate that song to woman number one on your list."

The young men's faces quickly changed from a smile to an uneasy stare. Chris continued. "Take song two and three and devote it to your little sisters, daughter, girlfriend, or aunt."

The boys were strongly displeased with Chris's suggestions. Isaiah spoke out first and was very upset. "Now why the hell would I dedicate any of those songs to my mom or daughter? I would whup somebody if they even play them songs in front of them."

Chris replied to the young man's comments. "I understand. Hold that thought, we are not done with the activity yet. Now I want ya'll to look at the videos you chose. Now I want you to replace the females in the videos with all the women on your list."

The room was quickly filled with "hell naws" and "f—— that's". Chris calmed the room down and asked the young men to explain why they were so upset. Mouse jumped up and was the first to walk into the trap that Chris had set for them. "Wait a minute, Chris. I thought you said this class was to teach us about how to treat a woman like you want your mom, sister, or daughter to be treated? If so, why would I want to put my mom or sister in a video where they are all naked and looking like some hoes?"

Chris stood up and shouted, "Exactly!" The young men were oblivious to why Chris had said that, but he began to explain. "You are supposed to learn to treat women like you would want a woman you love treated. But this is what you don't understand. All those women you are learning to lust after and to disrespect and call hoes and sluts and B's and telling to get in your car or telling that you wanna F them or throwing dollars at to get them to take their clothes off are all someone's mother, someone's sister, or someone's daughter. So why should your family members be any better? And I know what you are going to say. Well, they make they own choice to do all that. It's not my fault they doing all that," Chris stated as he mocked the young men's shot-down rebuttals.

"But what if your sister thinks that she has to be on the *Tip Drill* video for a guy to like her? What if she feels that she should let a man disrespect her or treat her like a hoe if he has money? 'Cause that's what you are showing them. You get mad at the thought of your loved ones being treated like this, but you treat others like this every day."

The young men were speechless. They had never viewed their actions in this light.

Chris continued, "Now let's talk about these heroes that you guys have. I want you to pretend that you are finding a husband for those women you love. I want you to raise your hand if you want your daughter to date your hero."

The boys looked like lost puppies as they looked around the room at the lack of anyone raising their hand. Chris persisted. "Oh, we don't have any takers, huh. Okay, now I want you to think about the description you gave of a female. How many want your loved one to be viewed by that description. Oh, once again, we have no takers, I see."

The young men began to drop their heads in shame. Their minds were going a million miles a minute trying to process this new awakening that Chris had put in their faces.

"Does anyone have anything to say?" Chris received no response. "Look, my young brothers, I'm not trying to make you feel guilty or judge you. That is not my goal at all. You have to learn these things. You have to learn that everyone is somebody to someone. Now I'm far from perfect. I have had plenty of times in my life where I could have had someone telling me this. I thought because I never disrespected girls then I was okay. Little did I know that I was disrespecting them all the time. I used to label girls 'hoes' just like the next boy. I used to look at the girls that were dressing like strippers. I used to—and sometimes still do—struggle with porn. I am still a man that struggles with lust. The only difference is I choose to fight it. Now I know that this may be foreign to you, but now is where the class truly begins. I'm not only going to show you how to look at females differently but to let your action show it. This is where you are going to take the journey from Boys to Gentlemen. Let me take a moment to really explain what I mean by *gentlemen*. It is far from just having manners or opening doors for ladies. Being a true gentleman means respecting a woman even when she shows none for herself. It means showing character, integrity, and discipline."

Several of the young men gave confusing looks. "Hey, Chris, can you give us the dumby version of the last things you said? You sound like my English teacher."

Chris laughed. "Sure, Mouse. Well, character and integrity go hand in hand. It is simply doing what you know is right when no one is looking. Even when you feel no one will know, you still do the right thing. Discipline is showing self-control. For example, when a girl is trying to get at you but you know that she is only doing it because she likes you and don't want you to think that she is stuck-up. You could use that to your advantage and let her do whatever you want. But then you know that you are taking advantage of her feelings. Discipline would be keeping yourself from taking advantage of her, even though she will let you and you could say that she wanted it."

The young men were a little unhappy with Chris's examples, and for a second, many of them thought that they may have bit off more than they could chew.

"Now, once again, this class is optional—so if you don't want to make this change, then you don't have to come. But if you want to learn, then all I ask is that you let me teach you. Like I said, I'm not perfect, so I will learn from you as well. I would be lying if I said that I didn't have the desire to watch those videos or listen to the music. The only difference is that I know that if I keep doing it, I will keep this world in the same condition when my children are born. So if you are with me on this, then raise your hand once again and not only say but truly accept the mission statement for this class. More than that, I want you to think of your loved ones as you take this oath."

The young men stood with a new understanding and took the oath with pride. This session with the boys was even more emotionally charged than the previous class.

"Now ya'lls homework for tonight is to think of how you have treated females in the past years, how you want to treat them, and I want you to write an apology letter to all those you have hurt."

Like always, Mouse needed further clarification of the task. "You mean we gotta write a letter to ALL of 'em? Every single one of 'em?"

Chris couldn't help but laugh. "No sir, Mouse. It's one letter apologizing to everyone."

Mouse gave a sigh of relief. "Good 'cause I don't think I got that much paper."

The other two classes followed with the same emotional charge and sense of conviction. For the first time, these young men were truly coming to understand the error of their ways. The thing that surprised Chris the most was that everyone was willing to acknowledge their actions as well as put forth the legitimate effort to learn something different.

As Chris began to walk to C hall, he had no idea that today he would play the role of the student and JC would be the teacher. As the two walked into the classroom, JC showed a maturity that hadn't been seen in him before. "Chris, I really been thinking about what you told me yesterday. I spent all night last night thinking of all the females that I've treated like trash. I also thought of how I learned to treat them like that. Now don't get me wrong. I'm not trying to pass the blame on anyone because, ultimately, it was my decision to act like I did. But at the same time, I had no one giving me a different option. But now that you have given me another option, I'm going to take it. Okay, what I'm trying to get at is that I am much more experienced at disrespecting females than you are. So I think I can give people an insight that you can't give them. I want to speak to the people in your class."

Chris was about to object, but JC cut him off.

"Look, Chris, I know what you are going to say, but what you are about to say is exactly why I should talk to them. I'm going to apologize to them for all of their family that I have hurt. This is for me, Chris. This is my chance to start making up for all I have done. And possibly help others to not fall in the same trap I did. You got a great message, Chris, and you deliver it great. But like I said, they will always see you as someone looking from the outside in."

Chris couldn't say a word. JC had given such a compelling argument that he had no choice but to consider it. "Okay, JC, I will try." All Chris could think about was how the young men would act when JC was brought in the class. It was almost as if people forgot that he was in the facility. After he had put JC back in his room, Chris walked to the control room and thought to himself. *Oh my, how am I gonna swing this. I don't know how these kids are going to act. And I can't afford for there to be any major behavior problems in the class 'cause it's still in the probation period. But I have to do this 'cause JC is right.*

Chris put his persuasive skills to the test and talked to his supervisor about JC speaking in the class. Needless to say, at first he was against it. "Now let me get this straight, Chris. You have gotten the kids to behave amazingly shortly after the most violent outbreak that we have had in JDC history, and you want me to let you take the kid that caused it all and put him in front of them to talk about an emotional subject? I got two words for you. Get out!"

"Wait, boss, hear me out. Since it has been so easy around here the past couple of days, nobody is calling in."

His boss began to laugh.

"No, but for real, boss. There are enough people to keep up with door checks and to have five DOs in the room. One for each kid. Plus, I think that after JC speaks to them, they will no longer be out for his blood. I really need you to trust me, boss. I will take full responsibility for this one."

Johnny was in a tight spot. It was a battle between his head, which was saying, "You would be a complete fool to do it," versus his gut that was telling him he could trust Chris. "All right, Chris, we are going to try this, but you got to promise me that if things go south, you get that boy out of there and get them kids calm."

"Now, Johnny, you know I'm gonna handle this side. I'm gonna go and let the other staff know. Oh yeah. Holley will definitely be on door checks."

Johnny simply laughed at Chris's remark. Chris went and asked his coworkers if they were okay with his plan. Once again, it was smooth sailing until he got to Holley. She felt the need to voice her opinion. "Your dang class ain't part of my job description. I'm not doing it."

Chris could only smile. "You are absolutely right, Holley. It would not be fair to ask you to do that, so you will just continue normal work operations while the others help with the class."

Holley's attempt to cause problems backfired on her. She had no comment, but her action spoke much louder than her words. Chris knew that she was going to be a problem, but he paid her no mind. The day was filled with surprises for Chris. When he walked to the halls to offer the good night prayer, the kids had a different plan for the night. "Hey, fellas, ya'll ready to pray."

One of the kids replied, saying, "Naw, Chris, tonight we gonna pray for you."

Chris was a little taken aback by the gesture. They all took the time to learn the Lord's Prayer and spoke it in unison. "All right, ya'll ready? Go. Our Father, which art in heaven, hallow it be thy name, thy kingdom come, thy will be done, on earth as it is in heaven. Give us this day our daily bread and forgive us our debts as we forgive our debtors. Lead us not into temptation, but deliver us from evil. For thine is the kingdom, the power, and the glory forever. Amen."

Tears had rolled down Chris's face. The young men had exposed a true weakness in him. It is one thing to love someone, but it is a totally different thing to be loved. And these boys loved Chris. This was something that he often tried to avoid acknowledging, but he was now put in a position where he could no longer ignore it. The repeated action in the other hall had no less of an effect on him.

Finally, he went to JC's door. When he opened it, JC was in his Bible. JC looked up from his Bible and asked Chris, "You ready to pray, sir?"

Chris smiled. "Yes, sir, I am."

"Chris, I wanted to tell you something before we pray. I was talking to my mom today in my visit about you. I wanted to tell you thank you. I've had a couple of men come in my life and try to play the father role, but they were all trying to use me. I can honestly say that you are the closest thing I ever had to a daddy. And if I had a daddy, I would want him to be just like you. I thank God for you, Chris."

The two of them prayed, and as Chris was walking out, JC had one last bomb to drop. "Hey, Chris. You are my hero, bro."

Chris had lost all composure by the time he locked JC's door. He went to the restroom to attempt to get himself composed only to be walked in on by JW. "What's wrong, son?"

Chris attempted to hide his tears and emotion, but it was extremely unsuccessful. "Nothing. I'm cool, Pops," Chris replied in a whimpering voice.

"Boy, so you just gonna lie to me like that. Ray Charles could see there is something wrong with you. Now what's going on?"

Chris cracked a smile. "Pops, I think these kids really love me."

JW responded quickly. "Of course they love you, boy. Some of these boys have never had anyone to ever tell them that they are anything but a failure. Now I care about these kids, but I can't give them what you give them. You give these boys hope. After they have been around you for some time, they really start to believe that they can do something with their lives. You are special, son. I have always told you that. There are few people on this earth that are built with a heart like yours."

Chris sat and listened. "Pops, JC just told me that I was his hero and I was the closest thing that he ever had to a father. It makes me feel good to know I was there for him, but it breaks my heart to think of how many boys grow up without a positive man in their lives."

JW placed his hand on Chris's shoulder. "That's why this class of yours is so important. These boys need this. Hell, I need this. I'm learning from sitting in your class, boy. You have a gift of reaching these kids. Don't let nobody stop you. As a matter of fact, I want to speak along with JC tomorrow if you will let me."

Chris had forgotten about that situation. "Oh man, you haven't even talked to JC yet, have you?"

"No, I haven't, but I'm gonna talk to him tomorrow."

Chris had found a new determination for his class. Before, it was just a good idea, but now it was an absolute need. After work Chris drove out to his grandfather's grave. He admired the flowers that had been left. He fell to his knees and began to speak to him. "Hey, Daddy. It was a wild day for me. Today, even more than before, I see how vital you were in my life. I'm teaching a class to the kids called From Boys to Gentleman. I'm just teaching them what you taught me. I told the kids about how you dusted all those other fathers in that race that one year. Oh, Daddy, there are so many kids out here without a father. I remember how you were always trying to take someone under your wing and give them some love. No one to teach them how to be a man. One of the kids in there told me that I was his hero and that I was the closest thing he ever had to a father. It felt good, but it hurt more that he had lived his whole life without a father. I know that I can't reach them all, but I'm gonna reach as many as I can. I promise, Daddy. I just want to tell you thank you for all that you did for me and for all you taught me. You were more than a dad. You were my best friend, and I will carry you in my heart for as long as it beats. Well, good night, Daddy." He bent down to kiss the headstone. "I love you, Daddy!"

I know that I'm writing this, but I'm ready to cry. This world has adopted the technique that Adolf Hitler used on the Jews. It's called dehumanization. Basically, he made the Jews seem like less than humans so his soldiers didn't feel bad about what they did to them. For example, if I tell you that the US Army killed five insurgents, you would probably have no problem with that. That's because in your mind, an insurgent is less than human. They are terrorist that are trying to destroy the USA. But if I tell you that the army killed five people that consisted of two mothers and three of their children, your emotional reaction to this is completely different.

This is no different than a man that labels a female as a hoe or slut. He is simply placing her in a category that will allow him to escape the guilt of his actions because if she was viewed as the beautiful queen that she is, then it's a terrible crime to treat her as the sexual toy that she is desired to be.

Yes, I understand that the girl has to learn to love herself, but that is the next book. Right now we are focusing on the male. We have to teach our young men to view females as queens, whether they act like it or not. Even the most promiscuous of men in this world do not want their loved ones to be treated like the women they defile each day.

Then there is my favorite response. "Well, she knows what I'm looking for, and she wants it too." I'm not trying to judge, and I know that everyone doesn't believe in the Bible and God. But for those of you that do claim to love the Lord, please explain to me what God says about premarital sex. Once again, I'm not judging 'cause I didn't make it until marriage either. But why wouldn't you try to be better than me versus using my mistakes as an excuse to fall in the same trap?

So, people, we now have a major issue that we can either sweep under the rug or we can address. The way I view it is that if we can begin to teach young men the value of women and the fine lost art of abstinence, we in turn will lower this amazingly high teen pregnancy rate that we have. This means we will have less young people attempting to raise babies. It means less children without a father. It means more little girls that aren't looking for the affection that they didn't receive from their father in the first boy that tells them they are pretty or that they love them. Which produces more young girls that respect themselves and don't have that baby at sixteen or younger. Are you following me? Let's give it a shot, people.

Chapter 11

We Are Overcomers by Our Testimonies

Many people miss out on their greatest chance to minister to others. It is one thing to tell people what they shouldn't be doing. It's another thing to give them an example. Many times we get so caught in the fear of people judging us or viewing us different that we don't tell people about our past struggles. We are quick to say that my past is none of their business. But what if our past is what will give them hope for their future?

Tomika and Erin came back to the church several times that week. They went to Bible study and choir practice. Today was a singles class. The pastor had asked them to come and speak at the class.

Tomika walked over to Erin. "Girl, I'm so nervous. What am I supposed to say? I just met God. How am I gonna tell these people about something I'm just learning about. What if they don't like me? What if they talk about me and judge me?"

Erin simply shook her head. "First of all, you know that if I give you anything, that I will give the truth. Baby, you have every right to be worried about everything that you just talked about. People will talk about you, and they will dislike you and they will judge you."

Tomika had a disturbing look on her face. She became extremely defensive. "Thanks, Erin. That is real comforting. I'm not going in there for them to just judge me. I'm tired of that. I'm trying to help them, and they are going to do me like that? Oh no, that's not gonna work. I have been judged and talked about enough. I'm not going to go give them more reasons to hate me."

Erin simply smiled and laughed at her, which made Tomika even more angered. "Erin, why are you laughing at me? This ain't funny!"

"Tomika, I'm laughing at what you just said. Do you remember reading about Jesus?"

Tomika nodded her head.

"Well, I want you to tell me what he did to deserve what they did to him. You have to know what this walk is all about. We won't be loved by everybody. This is what you have to know. Jesus is like an inside joke. Some get the joke and some don't. The people that get the joke laugh, but the people that don't get the joke get mad because they don't understand why you're laughing. People that don't really know that God is good don't want to hear others talk about how good he is. But you have to understand that your past is what shows God's glory. What he has brought you through allows them to not only hear but to see why we say God is so good. You have to know that right now you are closer to God than people that have been in the church for years. Your sincere heart, your love for him, and the faith you show is what makes your relationship so real.

"Tomika, you are amazing, girl, and you have an amazing story that will help so many. Now don't get me wrong. There are so many people that will love you and be so blessed by you, but I just don't want you to expect everybody to love you. Oh yeah. I didn't tell you, but the pastor wants you to speak to the young girls' group tonight. I told him that you would."

Tomika's eyes shot wide open. "Erin, why would you do that?"

"Girl, I did it because you have the chance to keep these lil girls from going through the things that you did. You have the chance to give these babies what you needed when you were in college."

Tomika went into a flashback of her years in college. She began to remember the pain and loneliness she felt. She remembered the nights she spent wishing that she would just die. That night at her house was not her first attempt with self-destruction. She had tried to cut her wrist and drink her pain into submission many times before that. Tomika fell to her knees and began to cry. She looked up to the sky and said, "God, I will do your will."

That afternoon the dynamic duo arrived at the church on a mission. They walked into the fellowship hall where the class was held. The ladies that were at church the past Sunday ran over to Tomika like she was a superstar.

One of the young ladies named Mica was the first to speak. "Girl, I don't think that you know how much you blessed me last Sunday. I was so excited when pastor said that you were coming today."

Erin just looked at Tomika and smiled. The meeting began. Mica got up and opened the meeting. "Today, we have a very special speaker with an amazing story. We are going to skip everything and just bring her up so she can have all the time that she needs. So with no further delay, I present to you Ms. Tomika Carter."

Tomika walked to the front of the class like a woman on a mission. She had been praying to God the whole way there about what she needed to do. Erin saw how she glowed with the anointing of God as she walked in front of the ladies.

"Hello, ladies. I'm so thankful for the chance to speak to ya'll. I'm just gonna give my testimony." Tomika began to go through her life from her childhood all the way to coming to church last Sunday. There was not a dry eye left in the room. At least one part of her testimony applied to every woman in that room.

The women began to ask questions. One of the young ladies named Monica was the first to speak. "Ms. Carter, how did you find the strength face to your son again?"

Tomika wasted no time responding. "Baby, it was God. I didn't have the strength. I felt less than human after I put my baby out on the street. I didn't know if he was dead or if he hated me. I felt like he should have hated me. I told Erin what I had done and expected her to leave my side and talk about how terrible of a mother I was, but all she did was pray for me. That night in my hospital bed, I called out to God for my son. And I tell you that my Jesus answered my prayer. My baby called me from the detention center, and for the first time, with a new understanding, we told each other that we loved each other. I praise God for that."

The next young lady to speak was Sharon. "Ms. Tomika, my question is for Ms Erin. Girl, how did you stay by her side after she kept pushing you away? I had a friend that I wanted to be there for, but when she shut me out, I just left her alone."

Erin stood up and spoke. "It was hard for me because at first I almost let the rejection get to me. But I knew that God had led me to her, so I prayed that God would make a way. It was the fact that I didn't leave and continued to love my sister that made me the instrument that God could use to reach her. Tomika always says that I saved her, but I know better. I was simply the vessel God used to bring her the blessings he had for her."

Janet was the next to speak her mind. "Ms. Tomika, I hear what you are saying, but I'm going to be real. I want a man. How have you dealt with not having a man in your life for so long?"

Tomika took a colder tone with that question. "You don't desire something that you despise. So many men hurt me that I put all men in that category. Even my son. Maybe God will send me a man one day, but I have learned the hard way that it is better to be alone with Jesus than to have a man that don't have Jesus. Now I know what you are talking about. I do miss the touch of a man holding me. And yes, I have needs just like any other woman, but that small pleasure was not worth the pain and destruction it caused in my life. You let God bring you a man, baby. You just start preparing yourself for the man you want. Sometimes we say we want a good man, but we are not putting out the right bait. I will tell you something someone told me. If you are trying to catch a monkey, you will put out a banana. If you are trying to catch a mouse, you will put out some cheese. If you want to catch an elephant, you are going to put out peanuts. You can't get mad if no monkeys come when you are putting out cheese. You can't get mad if no elephants come if you put out bananas. So how do we expect to attract a good man when we are putting out the bait to attract thugs and bums? Don't get mad at me. If it applies to you, just say ouch, and if it don't apply to you, then I ain't talking to you."

Every woman in the room gave a unanimous ouch. The women laughed and received Tomika's words well. Tomika looked in the group and saw a young lady with her hands over her heart and tears streaming down her face. Tomika knew the look on her face all too well. She walked over to her and grabbed the young lady's hand. "What's your name, baby?"

The young lady weakly whispered, "Brea."

Tomika could hear the pain in her heart. "What is it, dear? Talk to me please."

Brea looked up and let it poor out. "I feel like you have been talking directly to me all this time. Like you have been reading the pages of my life. It hurts so bad 'cause I just realized that I have been searching for the love of my father in man after man. I just want someone to love me. But all they want is sex. I tried to tell them that I didn't want to, but they used to tell me that I would do it if I loved them. I just wanted someone to love me. When I didn't have sex, the guys would ignore me. When I started having sex with all these guys, they started giving me attention and talking to me. It was cool for a min, until I went to this party with this guy I was dating.

"I really liked him. He told me that he loved me and that he would always protect me. That was all I wanted. That night he started drinking. He started taking my clothes off in front of everybody and started having sex with me in the middle of the room. I wanted him to stop, but he said, 'What's wrong, baby? I thought you loved me.' So I let him keep going. People started recording us and put it on the internet. The next day, he started ignoring me. When I finally caught up with him, I asked him why he hadn't been answering my calls. He acted like we were never even together. He put on a big show in front of his friends and said that we were never together and he was just drunk and wanted some. It broke me, Ms. Tomika. I had never felt hurt like that before. I just wanted to die.

"People kept calling me and harassing me. The school even got involved and put me on probation. I dropped out, and I have been fighting suicide for three weeks. I'm scared. I don't want to go to hell, but I feel like I'm already there. I don't even know why I came today because I was scared people are going to find out and put me out of the church. I don't want to do this no more."

Tomika looked into the young girl in her eyes and began to speak to her. "I know why you came today, dear. Baby, I remember being right where you are. I heard voices telling me to do it."

Brea began to cry even harder.

"So many men told me they loved me that I stopped believing in love. My daddy didn't love me, no man loved me, and I even tried to make myself believe that God didn't love me. But it's a lie, baby. God does love us. I don't even know you, but, Brea, I love you. I promise I do, and I will show you. God is going to allow me to show you."

Brea jumped from her seat and wrapped her arms around Tomika as the river of tears continued to flow. Tomika held her tight and told the other woman to come around as she prayed for the young woman's heart. Shortly after the women closed their meeting, it was time for Tomika and Erin to go to the youth meeting. Tomika was making up for lost time. She had not even become a member yet. When she walked into the gym, the first person she saw was May. The two of them ran to each other like long-lost friends. "Hey, beautiful, how are you doing, honey?"

"I'm great, Ms. Tomika. They told me that you were going to come speak to us. I'm so glad you are here. When you told your story at church, it really helped me."

Tomika stopped her. "No, baby, your poem was a blessing to my heart. If you didn't read that poem for anyone else in that sanctuary, you read it for me. Oh, May, I want to thank you again for your courage."

The meeting began and followed in the same fashion as the other one. Tomika told her story and touched the hearts of the young ladies. Tomika was truly doing God's will. Her testimony was giving these young girls hope. Tomika had felt alone before. She never knew just how many people were suffering from the same things that had tried to destroy her.

After the class, Tomika went to go visit with JC. She told him all about the meetings and the young ladies and how excited she was. JC began to cry as his mom spoke. Tomika grabbed JC's hand and said, "What's wrong, baby?"

There were two reasons for JC's tears. "Mama, I'm so happy for you and what God is doing in your life, and I'm proud of you. But it hurts me so bad to know what I have done to females. I may have been the person that made them feel the way you felt. I got to make it right, Mama. Today, Chris is going to let me speak to the boys in here so I can tell my story. I just wish I would have known, Mama. I just didn't know what I was doing to these girls. And what I was doing to myself and to my Savior. I got to make it right, Mama. I have to."

Tomika began to cry as well. "Son, I'm sorry that I didn't teach you. I know you didn't have your father, but I could have done so much more. I'm just as much to blame as you are. But we are not going to focus on blame. You go in there and you teach these young men, baby. Let your testimony give them hope for deliverance."

After the visit, JC was escorted back to his room. He started to think what he was going to tell everybody. For a second, he was scared of a repeat of the massive beating he received.

Just then, Chris came to the door. "Well, it's about that time, sir. Are you ready?"

JC nodded his head. He thought that Chris was talking about going to talk to the boys, but as he got ready to leave the room, JW walked in. JC never really talked to anyone except Chris, but unlike many of the other Dos, JW had never given him a reason to not like him. "Hello, JC. If you didn't know, my name is Julian." JW was extremely nervous. "Well, I need to talk to you about something. You see, when I was younger, I was just like you. I was the man. I had so many females and so many people trying to ride on my coattail. No one ever taught me anything about treating women right. As a matter of fact, my daddy taught me the exact opposite. He taught me that women were hoes and that they were just things to obtain like trophies.

"Well, a long time ago, I ran into this one girl that was different from all the rest. She was so amazing. She really caught my eye. She was fine, smart, and had goals. I really started to like her, but she was so into sports and school that she never even paid any attention to me. I never approached her because I was scared to get rejected. Well, it was senior year and they had a party on graduation night. This girl was so bad. I didn't see any other girl that night. Well, my boys caught me staring at her and they started calling me sprung and bet me that I couldn't bone her that night. I couldn't look like no punk in front of my boys, so I went over to her. We danced and talked all night, and the more she talked the, more I liked her. Like I said, she wasn't like those other girls.

"Well, after the party, we went to the lake and I had to do something that I didn't want to do to drop her guard. I told her that I loved her. As soon as I said that, we did the do. It was a great night for me, and I felt closer to her. Well, when I got home, my boys were there and they had already told my father about the bet. So he was equally interested in whether I had won the bet. When I walked in, they asked me if I did it and went back into my player mode and told them yes. They started calling people and spreading the word. My dad was so proud. I felt bad, but little did I know that I was about to feel a lot worse.

"The next day, she showed up to my house. Me, my dad, and my boys had just finished playing basketball. I tried to act like I didn't see her and just walked in the house, but she called my name. I walked over to her and she asked me if last night was real. She asked me if I loved her and why did I say it. I was in front of my dad and my boys, so I lied and I told her that I said it 'cause it sounded nice at the moment."

That phrase brought so much guilt to JC 'cause all he could see was Cherish.

JW continued, "she was so hurt. I will never forget her face while she stood in front of my house. I still haven't forgiven myself for that day, and I wish I could take it back. But I can't. I can only tell my story so others don't make the same mistake that I made. Do you understand me, son?"

JC said, "Yes, sir, I do. That's why I'm about to go tell these boys my story. Sir, I did almost the exact same thing to this girl named Cherish. I just wish I could take it back, but I know I can't. So I hope people will listen to what I'm telling them and what Chris is trying to teach them."

Julian saw his opportunity and he took it. "Yeah, son. You know that girl that you hurt? That's my daughter."

JC's heart dropped. He was so full of shame and couldn't say a word.

"She came to me and told me what happened, and I had to hold her and know that someone had done to her what I did to Tomika."

JC thought for a second. "Sir, did you say Tomika? Tomika what?"

Julian wasted no more time. "Yes, JC, it was your mom that I hurt. It was Tomika Carter. My name is Julian Ward. I don't know if she ever told you about me, but it was me, JC, and I'm so sorry. I will understand if you hate me, but all I ask is think about what you did to my baby."

JC could not move. He was so engulfed with a swarm of emotions that it paralyzed him. Finally he spoke, "I want to be mad, but I know why you did it. Now I just want to make things right. Sir, I'm so sorry for what I did to your daughter. I was so stupid. I'm just so sorry."

JW reached out his hand for a handshake. JC shook his hand. "JC, we are going to learn these boys something."

JC smiled. "Let's go get 'em, sir."

Chris was amazed at how smoothly it worked out. He looked at JW and JC and said, "I don't care what nobody say. Prayer works!"

Chris had made the opportunity for this to happen, but he had simultaneously made a huge mistake. Holley was in the control room. Usually, while Chris was talking with JC in his room, JW was in the control room. This kept Holley from listening in on their conversations. Without the intimidating presence of JW to discourage Holley from listening in, she took full advantage of her chance to gather info. About six of the kids had been released earlier that evening, so only nine remained for the class. The rest were brought to the dayroom for one big class. Chris opened the class with the mission statement. All the young men stated it with pride. This was the first time Holley was able to view the class for herself because it was in the dayroom. She was angered at the respect they showed for Chris and JW. Seeing it did nothing but fuel the flame of rage that burned at her very core.

Chris began to prepare the class for their guest speakers. "Well, fellas, raise ya hand if you did your homework."

All the young men were eager to share, but Chris had a different plan. "I'm glad you all did your assignment. Today we are going to have two guest speakers. Now before I bring out our first speaker, I need every one of you to read your letters to yourself."

The boys reflected off the words that they had written.

"Now I want you to give me your word that you will be on your best behavior."

Chris's request for them to behave created much intrigue to the young men about who these guest speakers were. Of course, you can count on Mouse to ask the question everyone is thinking and no one says. "Hey, Chris, why you asking us to behave like we been bad or something?"

Chris responded to the curious young man. "Mouse, this is a yes-or-no request. Stop giving me the tenth degree and just trust me. Like I said before, do I have yall's word that you will behave?"

The young men agreed with some hesitation. At that time, JW brought out JC. All the boys got silent as they saw him. They had not forgotten about their dislike for JC one bit, but they knew how important it was to keep their word. Chris was the last person these young men were willing to lose.

JC walked to the front of the dayroom. He was nervous because he could see the anger in everyone's face. He took a deep breath and began. "I want to apologize to everyone in here." That was the last thing any of the young men expected to hear. "I have hurt so many girls and women in my life that I have lost count. A little while ago, ya'll beat the breaks off of me. I don't remember the hits as much as I remember what ya'll said to me while ya'll hit me. Every one of you kicked and hit me because of some female that meant something to you that I hurt. I never thought about how I was hurting girls. I was just doing what Lil Wayne and almost every other rapper was telling me to do. I was getting them hoes. I lived a life that was equal to a lot of superstars. I had girls flockin' to me. At that time, they were just a face and a body to me. But now that I have been taught different, I will never disrespect another female like that.

"You see, those women that mean so much to you and that you would kill for were absent in my life. I didn't even have a real relationship with my mom. She was always working. I'm just now starting to understand what it is like to love a female like you are supposed to. I didn't know. But like Chris tells me, that explains what I did, but it doesn't excuse it. So I'm sorry for all of your loved ones that I hurt.

"But now I want to talk to you and give you a new view. I know Chris has been talking to ya'll, but I'm sure some of ya'll feel like Chris don't know what you are going through. Well, if you don't want to take it from him, then please take it from me. We have to learn to live this mission statement and not just say it. A lot of you hate me for what you do every day. If you tell the truth, a lot of you wanted to be like me or admired what I had until it was someone you cared about that I had. Some of you never did what I did, but it was only because you couldn't. If you felt like you could, then you may have been even worse than I was.

"I beg of you to listen to me. I have been there and done that. It's a terrible feeling at night when you wonder if a person will ever care about you for you and not for what you have or what you can do. Chris is the first person to ever help me and not look for anything back. He was real with me. Even when I disrespected him and cussed him out, he was there and just kept helping me. I don't know if ya'll have that in your lives, but I would have killed to have Chris when I was growing up. Like I told ya'll, I don't have no time machine. I can't go back and change what I have done, but maybe I can keep others from walking down the same road I went down."

JW stepped in and continued off what JC had said. "I'm telling ya'll that JC is right. I was a lot like JC when I was younger, and there is no worse feeling than fearing a boy is going to do to your daughter what you did to other girls. Well, my fear came true. Some guy did to my baby girl what I had done to so many other girls. I could only hold her and cry and tell her I'm sorry. I don't know if I was saying sorry to her or to all the women I had hurt 'cause now I truly knew their pain. I'm telling you.

Young men, please don't ignore what we are telling you. You no longer have the excuse that you didn't know. I know it is hard. I'm not gonna lie to you. But doing what is right is rarely easy when you haven't been taught. Even when you have been taught, it is still hard to do what's right. Well, I'm not gonna take up any more of your time. Back to you, Chris."

Chris looked at the small group of young men and saw the conviction on their faces. "Well, does anyone have anything they want to say?"

Isaiah stood up and spoke. "When Chris made us do that activity with the songs and videos, that really opened my eyes. I think I would lose my mind if my lil girl was on that video. While Chris was walking through the hall today, I was telling him about my baby girl, and he asked me was I being a man that I would want her to be with. I said no. But that hurt me so bad. So, Grandpa, I know just what you are saying. I'm scared that day will come for me that my baby comes to me and tells me that somebody hurt her like I hurt some girls. And, JC, I'm not gonna lie. I thought you was one of the flyest dudes walking until you hurt my lil cousin. I was trying to be like you on the cool.

"I remember I heard some girls talking about you and how stupid girls were for trying to talk to you and throw themselves at you. Right after they said that, I walked up to them and told them that they was some stuck-up hoes and to quit hating. They was only saying that 'cause they wanted to be with you. Later that day, one of the girls came up to me and asked me if I really thought that she was stuck-up. I told her yeah. She asked me how she could change that. I told her to let me and my boy run a train on her. She let us do it. We took her virginity, and that's how I got my lil girl. I'm scared for the day she asks me how me and her mom met. So I guess I'm saying I'm sorry too and you cool with me, bro. I just want to be a better man for my baby girl. But I know now that I have to understand that all the other girls I talk to are someone else's baby girl. I see what you are saying, Chris. I got you, Pops."

Mouse followed. "Yeah, JC, I must admit that I thought you was tight until you did that mess to my sister. But when I heard about you doing the stuff to other girls, I didn't know I was laughing and giving you your props. I didn't care until it hit home. This really helped me see on a new level what Chris was talking about. I ain't got no daughter yet, but I'm gonna treat them girls like I want someone to treat my sister. So I'm sorry, and I'm cool wit you too, JC."

All the young men accepted JC's apology. JC had a challenge for the young men. "Look, ya'll, it's up to us to not only change but spread the word. Chris and JW done put a lot of work in us, so now it's up to us to finish the class and learn how to treat a woman. We already know how not to treat them, but we still need some teaching. So now that ya'll ain't trying to kill ya boy, can I get in the class with ya'll?"

They all laughed and welcomed their once sworn enemy into the group.

Chris leaned against the wall with his arms folded. "Ya'll are amazing. I'm so proud of ya'll. I think we have had enough of class for today. I'm gonna go ask boss if ya'll can have free time."

Chris walked to Johnny's office and knocked on the door. Johnny swung the door open. He was scared that the plan had gone south and part two of "whup JC" had begun. "What happened? Did they jump on him?"

Chris laughed. "No, boss. Everything went great. We finished with class early, so I wanted to know if we could give the kids free time."

Johnny took a deep breath of relief. "Man, you scared the crap out of me. They really cool?"

"Yeah, boss, they are all in the dayroom now."

"Well, if they are all cool, then yeah, they can have free time."

Chris walked back to the dayroom and informed them that they were on free time. Even though they were on free time, all they did was talk about the class and the experiences they had. Johnny walked out and saw how the kids were behaving and called Chris into the control room. "Man, Chris, I'm gonna call the president. You should get the Nobel Peace Prize for this stuff you doing."

Holley heard what Johnny had said, and that was the final straw for her.

It is simple. It is hard to take advice from someone that doesn't know your struggle by experience. Chris was opening the door for these young men, but part of his message was still questioned because he had not walked their path. So he was still viewed as a partial outsider. You don't want to talk to someone about an alcohol problem that has never taken a drink in their life. You wouldn't feel like they could understand you. You would feel judged. That is why it is so important for us to give our testimonies. The Word says in Revelation 12:11, "And they overcame him by the blood of the Lamb, and by the word of their testimony; and they loved not their lives unto the death." So don't sit on this power. Tell your story to give God glory.

Chapter 12

Misery Loves Company

Amazing things are happening. The class has superseded Chris's expectations in just a few days. These young men were so open-minded and open-hearted. They only lacked direction. Chris was able to show a masterful combination of advice, information, understanding, tough love, motivation, compassion, and possibly the most important, trust. By him trusting JW and JC, he was able to intensify the effectiveness of his message exponentially.

Tomika has walked into her calling. Each day she is getting closer to God. Her testimony has made such an impact on so many people. She has met her first true friend in Erin. Erin has taught her what love is, and because of her new knowledge she was able to truly love her son.

JC has obtained a healthy relationship with a male. He has someone he can trust and has begun to guide him. Both he and Julian have begun to make up for their past actions by taking the preventive route. Johnny is simply happy that the detention center is not on riot alert. Everyone seems to be doing well but Mrs. Holley.

The worst thing you can do to a person that is absolutely dependant on attention is to ignore them. This is exactly what Chris had done. Even worse than that, he had caused others to ignore her. All of her usual partners in crime were enjoying the fruits the class produced far too much to allow her to administer her daily dose of drama. The class had made everyone's job a breeze. Holley was the woman that the kids used as an excuse to treat females the way they did. She had no respect for herself. She needed attention in any way she could get it. The number one need she had was to feel sexy. This was the root of her hatred for Chris. He had called her out for trying to make passes at him and others despite the fact she was married. He also got into an altercation with her where he saw her wearing inappropriate clothing and making sexual remarks to the kids. A few of the kids even went as far to say that she had slept with them outside of the facility. Once Chris had embarrassed her in this private conversation, she had silently sworn vengeance on him. Holley was a very dangerous person. She had no limits on what she would do to get her revenge. To say that she was unhappy with the lack of attention she was receiving would be about as much of an understatement as saying hurricane Katrina did little damage to New Orleans. She was on the war path. She had put together a plan to destroy all that Chris had been working on. The first step required a couple of phone numbers from JC's visitation file. Step two would be easy since all the workers cell and home numbers were on the call roster. The third step would involve a couple of meetings behind closed doors with people higher in the chain of command. The rest of her plan would depend on what adjustments she would have to make.

Two weeks later, Tomika and Erin went to lunch with the pastor and his wife. The pastor was more than pleased with the work the two young ladies had done for the kingdom but had some urgent advice from the Lord for them. They met at a hole-in-the-wall Mexican restaurant that may have been Eneilaba's best-kept secret. The pastor opened the meal with a prayer and then began with his assignment. "Ladies, you have been nothing but a blessing for me and the church. Your spirits are phenomenal. I'm telling you that ya'll will be blessed beyond reason. But I must give you the message that God has given me to give to you."

The ladies were quite frightened with the thought of this message from God.

"Tomika, you have found your way to God. You are so driven and sincere with your determination to do his will. You have found yourself at night waking up just to pray or to sing his praises. You have learned the true meaning of tears of joy. You have been praying to God to be closer to him. You don't know what it is, but you have been asking God to show you what is standing between you and him. Just last night, you told God that you will never turn your back on him."

Okay, it was official. Tomika was spooked. She was unable to understand how on point the pastor was with what he was telling her. She politely interrupted him. "Wait a second, Pastor. Do you have a video camera in my house or something? How do you know this?"

The pastor calmly replied, "God."

She still couldn't explain it, but she knew he was telling the truth.

The pastor continued, "Tomika, you are so in love with God that the thought of disobeying him brings tears to your eyes and a burning in your chest. But I must tell you this. There is a storm in your life that you have been running from for years. It's an anger and rage that you have that is so strong that if you don't deal with it before it comes to you, it will cause you to turn your back on God."

Tomika immediately became defensive. *There is nothing that I will let come between me and God. Nothing. I have spent too long away from him to ever turn my back on him*, she thought to herself.

"I know that you feel there is nothing that can make you turn your back on God, but I'm telling you, Tomika. This is something that will affect every aspect of your life if you don't stop running from it and deal with it. It could cause you to make actions that will affect your ministry forever. Now if I'm wrong about this, then I'm just a fool and you can call me the liar I am. But if I'm right—which I promise you I am—then you may never forgive yourself for not taking action."

Tomika sat there attempting to grasp the mountain of a burden that had just been placed on her. "Well, sir, what is it?"

The pastor looked straight into her eyes and said, "Him."

Tomika knew at that very second of whom the pastor was speaking of. She got up from the table and began to walk down the street. Erin was stuck to her seat. She was afraid of what the pastor was going to tell her.

"Dear Erin. Yes, I do have a message for you as well."

Erin felt intrigued and a little violated at the same time. "Pastor, are you like a mind reader or something? Do you hear me saying these things to myself, or are you just guessing?"

The pastor laughed. "Yes, ma'am, I hear your thoughts. I'm operating in my prophecy gift, and the Holy Ghost is allowing me to hear your thoughts, but that is not important right now. I have a message for you. You have become a protector for Tomika, but you will not be able to protect her from what is about to happen. Tomika's storm is coming, and she will either concur it or let it consume her. All you can do is pray for her strength and not try to act out of your emotions. Your job is to sit still no matter the outcome."

Erin stayed in her seat for three hours, trying to absorb all that she had been given. After coming back to her senses, she grabbed her phone and called Tomika. "Girl, where are you?"

Tomika was hesitant in giving up her location but finally gave in. "I'm at the lake. I need some time, Erin. I'm okay, I promise."

Erin did not believe her at all, but she remembered the pastor's words and was obedient. "Okay, Tomika. I love you, girl!"

"I love you too, Erin. Bye." Just as Tomika got off the phone with Erin, she received a call from a number she did not recognize.

Chris had been spending many nights telling Lisa about the class and everything that had happen. "Baby, all last week we did exercises to show the kids how to deal with the peer pressure that they will face. They learned that whenever someone comes up to you and asks you to do something that you know is wrong to another female, you ask them if that is something you would want me to say to your sister or cousin. Oh, baby, these kids are amazing, and they are really committing themselves to this. People always say that this is a lost generation, but I think that we are about to find it."

Lisa was captivated with these events. "Dang, baby. This is better the *Young and the Restless*, *Jerry Springer*, *Dr. Phil* and *Oprah* combined. I'm so proud of you, boo. You are doing an amazing thing with these kids. These boys needed you. Don't let anyone discourage you."

The young lady was such an inspiration to Chris. Her words never fell on deaf ears when she spoke to him. It was time for work once again, but something just didn't feel right.

As Chris entered the building, he saw Holley walking out of the superintendent's office. She gave him a devilish grin as she walked to the back. JW walked in the door shortly after him and was not happy at all. He stormed in and walked past Chris as if he didn't know him. Chris called to him out of concern. "Hey, Pops, hold up. What's the deal wit you?"

JW was enraged. Chris had not seen him this upset since one of the kids spit in his face before they restrained him. Chris called to the control room from the front desk and let them know that he and JW had a situation that they needed to take care of and would be in shortly. The two of them walked back to his car. "Okay, Pops, you are gonna have to let me know what's going on."

JW began to explain. "So I'm getting ready for work today and Cherish comes home early. She walks in crying and asked me how could I do it. I had no idea what she was talking about, so I asked her to explain. She said that she got a call at school and some lady told her that I found out what JC had done and I beat him so bad that he had to go to the hospital. Then she says that, out of retaliation, I went and did the same thing to his mom. I told her it wasn't like that at all. Then she cut me off and said, 'Daddy, tell me the truth. Did you hurt JC's mom or not?' I couldn't lie to her so I told her, 'Yes, I did, baby, but that was a long time ago.' But before I could get out anything other than yes, she ran off. I know that Holley called my baby. It's one thing to do what she does at work, but she brought this mess to my daughter. Oh, but her tail is mine now."

Chris attempted to calm his mentor down. "Now hold up, Pops. What you gonna do, go choke her out in the control room so you can go to jail? You need to calm down."

JW exploded. "Don't give me that calm down crap, Chris! Because of this chick, my baby girl is gone somewhere not answering her phone and not speaking to me! My baby ain't ever looked at me like that. Chris, before for she ran out, she said she doesn't know if she will ever forgive me for this. If this was an average teenager, then I would just count it as hormones. But this is the most mature lil girl I have ever seen in my life. She didn't tell me that because she was mad. She said it because she meant it."

Chris was having a hard time playing the mediator because he was getting more upset by the second. "Look, Pops, I understand, but you can't go in there and do nothing stupid. I'm gonna go tell Johnny you have a family emergency. Go find Cherish and try to explain this to her. But before you do anything, just sit here for a second and get yourself together."

JW agreed to Chris's request. Chris walked in to Johnny's office to explain what was going on with JW. "Hey, boss, JW has got a family emergency that he has to deal with."

Johnny had just got off the phone. "Chris, have a seat."

"Okay, boss, what's up?"

"I just got off the phone with the superintendent. I'm gonna have to place you and JW on suspension until this investigation is over."

Chris was flabbergasted. "Until what investigation is over?"

"Somebody has went to the chief and said that you and JW had a relationship with JC before he came in here that ya'll didn't report it. They said that JW was dating JC's mom and JC was dating Julian's daughter, and that you knew about it and allowed JW to organize the riot because of what JC had done to JW's daughter."

Chris jumped up and slammed his hands against the table. "That's all bull and you know it, Johnny. That is not what happened."

Johnny tried to explain his position. "I believe you, Chris, but my hands are tied. I have to send you home and you can't come back until the investigation is over. Just between me and you, I know that this is all bull, and I'm gonna do everything in my power to get this cleared up so you can keep your job. I need you to keep it cool and just wait this one out."

Chris's concerns went far past the suspension. "It's not about this job, Johnny. What about my boys? What about the class? I'm really getting to these kids. I can't leave them right now."

Johnny smiled. "I was already thinking about that. You are a certified church volunteer. And today happens to be Wednesday. You can come and do your class at seven. You can't come to work, but there are funny exceptions when it comes to religion."

Chris walked out the office and by the control room. As he walked by, he saw Holley. She looked at him and blew him a kiss. It took every ounce of strength he possessed in his being to refrain from walking in the control room, hawking a luggy from the deepest part of his belly, and dislodging it from his mouth on a one-way collision course with her face followed by a backhand that would make A Pimp Named Slickback proud. Little did he know the true need for his strength was waiting for him outside.

JW was still outside trying to get his head together. Chris did not want to add any fuel to his flame with his newfound information. He was sure that it would send JW over the top. As he began to walk toward JW, a cab pulled up. Seconds later, an enraged Tomika bolted from the back door. She made a beeline straight for JW. She simply yelled, "Julian Ward!"

As JW looked up, he was welcomed with a fist. Chris grabbed Tomika as she began to shout, "You bastard. It's one thing to hurt me, but you hurt my son. What the hell is wrong with you, putting your hands on my child like that?"

Chris was in the middle of a situation that he would not wish on his worst enemy. Chris shouted, "JW, get out of here now!"

JW paused for a second, remembering the day he left Tomika on that sidewalk. He felt like he deserved whatever Tomika wanted to do to him, but her current reason for attacking him was over a lie. So he took Chris's advice and ran to his car and drove off. As Chris held on to the hysterical mother, he was all out of ideas. He saw that her screaming was about to draw a crowd that would only make the situation worse. So he did the only thing that came to his heart. He looked up and at the top of his lungs screamed, "JESUS!"

Tomika froze instantaneously. Chris walked her to his car and put her in. He walked over to the cab and gave him 30$ and told him to keep the change. The cab driver gave Chris the money back and said, "Naw, bro, you keep that. I'm just glad she not getting back in the car with me. You be careful. She hit that dude like Tyson in the 90s."

Chris ran back to his car and drove off. He tried to speak to her, but she was in a trance. All she could hear was the words of her pastor. She felt like Peter when Jesus told him that he would deny him three times. She was so hurt that she had lost herself like that.

Finally Chris was able to get her attention. "Ma'am, will you please tell me what happened back there? Why did you do that?"

Tomika's eyes began to fill with tears. "I was at the lake trying to deal with a situation that has held me captive for years. I was forcing myself to be vulnerable with what I was feeling and I got a phone call. Some woman that says she was calling me because she couldn't take it anymore. She said that she overheard one of the workers at her job bragging about how he had arranged for my son to get jumped and how he got his licks in. She said that it was over his daughter. Then she told me that his name was Julian Ward. I don't know if you know what happened between me and Julian."

Chris interrupted her. "Yes, ma'am, I do. And let me tell you that Julian has not forgiven himself since that day. JC getting jumped had nothing to do with Julian, I promise you. The kids jumped him because all the females JC had hurt were someone special to them. Please trust me. Ask JC. Just the other day, Julian told me about what he had done to you and how he had to make it right. Almost the exact same thing that he did to you, JC did to his daughter. Julian told JC what he had done to you and that he now knew that JC was the one that hurt his daughter. They both spoke in my class and really helped the kids."

Tomika recalled JC telling her about another worker that really helped him out, but he wouldn't tell her the name. "I believe you, Chris. I'm so sorry for acting like that. I know this sounds crazy, but I need to talk to Julian. I need you to trust me. I'm not going to do anything crazy. He is the last thing standing between me and God. I'm sure of it."

Chris looked at his phone and dialed Julian's number. "Hey, Pops. Look, I know this may sound a little weird, but Ms. Tomika wants to meet with you."

Surprisingly, Julian was completely willing. "Bring her to my house. I'm waiting on her."

Chris drove her over to Julian's house and dropped her off. He had a peace about the situation that he had no time to question. It was six forty-five and he had to get back to the detention center for church. He pulled up at six fifty-eight and busted a full sprint to the door and rang the buzzer.

Holley answered. "May I help you?"

Chris replied out of breath. "Yeah, I'm here for church."

"Oh, okay, I will send someone right out to get you."

One of the other workers came to let him in. As he walked past the control room, Holley was more than shocked to see Chris walk past. She quickly jumped on the phone only to hear the voicemails of the people she was trying to reach. Chris walked to the front of the dayroom and began to prepare for the class. Holley was hotter than fish grease at fish fry on the Fourth of July. Chris made all efforts not to look at her. The boys were brought out and they were super excited to see who was leading church.

Mouse was the first to come out. "Aww man, Chris, where you been? Holley told us that you quit and wasn't coming back."

Chris had not been this mad ever in his life. He was usually cool, calm, and collected, but his effort to hide his frustration was ever so evident. "Naw, boy, I ain't quit. I'm sure she was just playing with ya'll."

The rest of the kids that had chosen to sleep in for church had a change of heart when they caught wind of who was leading the service. There were a couple of new intakes that didn't even know Chris but were curious from all that they had heard from the others.

After all the kids were there, Chris quickly opened with prayer. "Dear God, I thank you for every moment that I have spent with these young men. I praise you for the growth you have blessed me to observe in them. I pray that you let them know that I love them. I pray that you open their hearts and minds to receive what I have to give them. Let your spirit move in this place. God, I pray you give me the peace that passes all understanding and the wisdom to see your purpose in the storm that I am in. Thank you, God. Amen."

Chris was in tears 'cause part of him knew that this may be the last time that he ever got to teach his class here.

"Well, fellas, this is the last day of From Boys to Gentlemen. I could not be prouder of you. You boys have taken this class and made it your own. Now it's one thing to do the class in here, but what will you do when you feel no one is looking? How will you act when ya boys are pressuring you or calling you a punk or scared 'cause you aren't doing what they want you to do?"

Mouse raised his hand and answered, "I'm gonna tell them no. I'm gonna tell them that I wouldn't want nobody to do that to my sister. And I'm gonna ask him if he would want somebody to do that to his mom, sister, or future daughter. 'Cause that chick—I mean that young lady—that you want me to disrespect is someone's daughter or sister and will be someone's mother one day."

Chris could no longer hold it in. He began to cry. The kids were completely concerned. Chris explained his tears. "No, fellas. I'm crying because I'm so proud. I'm not gonna lie. I didn't know if ya'll would take this serious, but now I know. Now I see. I just want to say thank you. Thank you for all you have taught me."

The boys were still unable to get past the emotion Chris showed. Several other kids began to cry, and they didn't even know why. "Man, Chris, I don't like this. This sounds like you telling us good-bye. Are you quitting on us? Did somebody offer you a new job? What's the name of the company so I can call and get you fired?"

Chris laughed at Mouse's colorful comment. "Look, fellas, I'm not gonna lie to you. I don't know if I will be back, and why doesn't matter. But ya'll are in my prayers. And I will never forget ya'll. I want ya'll to focus on getting out of here so ya'll can live ya'lls lives."

The boys were unhappy with Chris's statement but respected his undying honesty with them. "We love you, Chris. No homo!"

Chris finished up with some scriptures and another prayer. As Chris was escorted out, the boys stood up and recited the mission statement as a tribute to their father figure. Several of his coworkers tried to pump him for more info about what was going on, but he politely kept them in the dark as he walked to his car.

Holley was out on a smoke break as he walked to the car. He walked up and stood next to her. She looked at him as she blew a large cloud of smoke in his face. "What the hell do you want, Chris? Don't even waste your time asking me about anything 'cause I don't know nothing about any of that mess."

Her unprovoked lying gave more verification that she was responsible for today's circus-like events. In only thirty seconds, Chris's brain flashed over two hundred hateful and demeaning things to say to her. Not to mention that they were in a blind spot for the cameras so there would be no video evidence if he pushed her into a wall and said that he tripped. But on second thirty-one, he heard a voice that said, "I give you peace." At that moment he had no anger or frustration toward her at all. He actually felt convicted by the very lessons he taught. Even when a woman doesn't act like a queen, you take it upon yourself to treat her like one and let her know that she is a queen. He turned away and walked to his car. As he closed the door, he looked at his phone and he had three missed calls from Pops.

Dang. That girl Holley should be working for the government as a spy. She really came up with a plan. But once again, this is what happens when you are trying to do something good with your life. You would be an absolute fool to think that everyone is just going to pat you on the back all the way to the top. You better be ready for some of them pats to be exchanged for some stabs. The sad thing in this is when you know that you are doing right. When the devil sees you as a threat, he will do whatever he can do to keep you from reaching that goal, whether it is to discourage you, discredit you, or simply flat out try to destroy you. Holley is a confused and bitter woman. She is an addict and attention is her fix. If I know my readers at all, ya'll are ready for Holley to get beat up, stabbed, shot, and hit by a train in this next chapter. Now dealing with Tomika before she got saved, you would have gotten all those actions. She would have simply substituted the train for Chevy Tahoe. But let's see what a saved Tomika does, shall we?

Chapter 13

Blessing or Curse? Only Time Will Tell

A young man has been praying for a car for months but can't get any dealership to finance him. Then he runs into this guy that sells him a great car for a super low price. If I stop there, this sounds like such a blessing. But the car that the guy sells him was stolen. Now the young man is out of all his money and has no car. Things are not always what they seem. Another scenario. A young girl is attempting to sneak off with some friends to go to a party with some college guys that they have never met. While she is crawling out the window, her dad pulls up and sees her. Now this has got to be a curse, right? She is going to be so grounded and possibly beaten. There is no way that any good can come out of this, right? Well, it just so happens that the party her friends went to was a gang-initiation party. All her friends were repeatedly raped by men in masks. This is a very rough way for me to tell you that sometimes what we view as a blessing is really a curse, and what we view as a curse is really a blessing.

Tomika's heart was about to beat out of her chest. As she walked up to the door, her legs felt like she had just ran the New York marathon in high heels. Though she was greatly fearful, she was equally determined to deal with this storm. She knocked on the door, but there was no answer. After about five minutes, Tomika was far past upset. *This dirty bastard stood me up*, she said to herself.

Just as she was about to take her long walk home, Julian pulled up to the house. He had found Cherish, but she was still not talking to him. She was still under the impression that Julian had done the things that she heard. Instead of trying to argue with her, he simply brought her back to meet Tomika. The three of them gave silent stares as JW motioned them toward the house. They walked into the kitchen and sat at the table. Tomika thought for years what she would do and say if she was ever put in this position, but nothing was coming to her. She sat there so quietly.

After about five minutes of listening to the lights hum, Tomika finally broke the silence. "Why did you do that to me, Julian? Why?" The tears began to flow as she inquired for her much-deserved explanation.

Julian could not look at her. He began to stare at his hands as he explained. "Tomika, I swear I didn't mean to. I was so young and dumb. The truth is, I think I did love you. My boys was clowning me 'cause they caught me staring at you that night. I didn't want to hurt you, but I was scared that I would lose my rep and, worse than that, my father's respect. He taught me to be a player. He always told me to never catch feelings for these... girls. A real player never catches feelings. He was always trying to push me to be something that I wasn't. To tell you the truth, you were my first. All the other girls just said they did something with me 'cause I was so popular. I never denied it, so I got a reputation as a player."

JW began to lose the battle with the tears that he had been fighting since he had started. "To tell you the truth, you were the only girl I ever actually wanted to make love to. I slept with so many women after you, but none of them meant anything. I was blessed with Cherish because her mom dropped her off at my doorstep like it was a movie. You was special for me, Tomika. I just let the peer pressure get the best of me. I know that is no excuse, but I'm so sorry. I'm so, so sorry."

JW lost it and began to cry like a baby. Tomika felt as if an eagle had swooped down and pulled her very soul from a fire of torment. So many times before, she felt as if she longed for only revenge. But she dared to say at this moment that she was free. "I wanted revenge. I wanted you to feel pain. I wanted to hurt you like you hurt me. I must have played this day over a billion times in my head. What I would say to you and what I would do to you. I have killed you so many times in my heart. I always felt like you didn't even care what you did to me. I just want to say thank you. Not for the apology but the opportunity to forgive you. Now I can go to a new level in my sweet Jesus."

Tomika began to lift her hands in praise as she screamed out the mighty name of Jesus. JW was still trying to get past the comment she made about killing him in her heart many times. Even though he was still a little scared, his happiness for Tomika far outweighed the fear. He had been forgiven and that was a liberation that only she could give.

As Tomika continued to praise, Cherish walked over to her father with tears in her eyes. "Daddy, I'm so proud of you. I know it was hard for you to open up like that. I'm sorry that I didn't believe you."

Julian fell to his knees, grabbed Cherish, and held her as tight as he could without hurting her.

Chris began to panic when he saw the missed calls. He rushed over to Julian's house and ran toward the house. He busted through the door in time to see Tomika dancing, yelling, and crying while Julian and Cherish were on the floor in their own tearful embrace. He had no idea what to think. So he stood there shocked for a second, trying to grasp a better understanding of what was going on.

Finally Cherish looked up and saw Chris and ran to him with much excitement. "Hey, friend. What are you doing here?"

Chris used this opportunity to get clarification. "Hey, baby girl, did she cut your dad or something?"

"No, Chris. Daddy apologized to her and she said she forgave him. Daddy just fell to his knees and started hugging me."

This was a sight to behold. A couple of hours later, they all sat at the kitchen table. Tomika began to tell her journey. This was so helpful for Cherish to hear. "Hey, Daddy, can we go to church with her this weekend?"

Julian had not been to church since he was in high school. "Okay, baby, I guess we can go."

With all that had went on in the day, Chris forgot to tell JW that they were suspended. "Oh, JW, man, I got some bad news. We are suspended from work because we are under investigation."

Julian's head popped up. "Investigation for what?"

"Well, Holley went to the chief and told him that we organized JC getting jumped. They also know about JC and Cherish. I don't know how this is going to turn out, Pops."

"Shoot I know how it is going to turn out. I'm gonna go find another job. Investigation or no investigation, it is time for me to move on. I love those kids, but I need to start following my dreams. Some of my boys from college have been trying to get me to go into business with them for a long time."

Chris was a little thrown by the statement. "That's good for you, but what about me?"

"Chris, you are a smart young man with all kinds of talents. You will find another job before I will."

Chris began to get frustrated. "I know I can find another job, but what about the kids? We are just gonna leave them like that?"

Julian sighed. "Hey, it might sound bad, but yeah. I have put in my work, son. Like I said, I love those kids, but I still have a life to live. I'm not trying to save the world. Now I will still do my part to help others, but I don't need that job to do it."

Chris was far less than pleased with Julian's view on the kids. He walked out to his car. Just before he got in, Tomika grabbed his hand. "Look, Chris, I know you don't know me and you might think I'm crazy, but I have to tell you this. What the devil means for our bad, God means for our good. I don't know what that means in your situation, but I think that is what God is giving me to tell you."

Chris received no comfort from her statement. All he could think about was his kids. He had already convinced himself that he had worked his last day there. He went home and played his Xbox for the rest of the night. For several days, he waited by the phone for his job to call. Finally they called him in for a meeting.

Chris walked through the front doors and told the clerk that he was there. Shortly after, the chief came out to greet him and called him back to his office. "Well, Mr. Daughtery, I must be honest. We don't want to let you go. You have made such an amazing impact on the kids in the facility. But due to the fact that we saw you, JW, and JC's mother outside fighting, we have no choice but to acknowledge the possibility of foul play. We also have interviewed your coworkers and some of them informed us that you would enter the young men's rooms for long periods of time. Is this true?"

Chris said yes.

"Well, Mr. Daughtery, I thank you for your honesty and that does nothing but make my decision harder. Due to the speculation of an unprofessional work relationship and the incident in front of the building, I'm faced with a choice that I must make. We are going to have to terminate you."

Chris's heart dropped. He made no attempt to argue. He stood and shook the chief's hand and walked out the door before the tears escaped his eyes. He understood why he was being fired, and even though the way he was presented was false, it didn't change the fact that he was breaking the rules. The position that he put himself and his coworkers in could have gone south at any moment. He did constantly put himself in harm's way by going into the kids' rooms. This was a new type of pain for him. It was one thing to leave on your own terms, but it's totally different when you feel like something is being ripped away from you. Things got ugly once word got around that JW and Chris had been fired. The kids began to show out daily. Some of the other workers were almost as upset as the kids were.

It did not take long for Holley to be put on the chopping block. She received threat after threat from the kids. No one really cared, but Holley's life was hell. Her husband was talking about leaving her, and she felt like her children didn't love her because they always asked for their father. It was revealed to her that her husband found out about her cheating. He had begun to see another woman and had been bringing Holley's kids around.

She was sitting on the couch one evening on her day off, and her son came up to her and said, "Mom, I want to go stay with my other mommy. I don't want to stay with you anymore."

Holley ran to her husband and asked him what the young boy was talking about. He told her about the other woman and how he knew she had been cheating. He even went as far as to tell her that he knew that their two oldest children were not even his. He was going to divorce her, and she would not get a dime from him because he could prove that she had been unfaithful. She was a mess and had reached her breaking point.

Later that evening, there was a female intake at work. Holley was performing the procedures of this intake. The young girl was a fiery one. She cursed up a storm from the second she came in the door. After the paperwork was finished, the young lady was walked back to the shower and her room. She had already developed a strong dislike for Holley. While in the dayroom during free time, Holley lost it. She attempted to tell some of the kids to be quiet, and they ignored her. Not only did the kids ignore her, but the other DOs offered her no assistance. The new young lady stood up and told her what she could do and where she could go. (Use your imagination and fill in the blanks of that open puzzle.) That was the final straw.

Holley and one of the other female DOs escorted her to her room for that outburst. Right as the door was opened, Holley pushed the young girl and started punching her in her face. The young girl proved to be much more than Holley was ready for and began to return fire. Instead of the other DO pulling Holley off the girl, she was pulling Holley away to safety. Holley ran to the restroom and locked herself in the stall. She had truly reached rock bottom.

Some of the other workers were concerned about what was about to happen with the kids. There were several rumors of another riot and other actions that would have DOs as the target of attack. They came together and thought of a plan. During the visitation period, kids either received a phone call or a visit. But due to the amount of behavioral problems that had occurred since the departure of JW and Chris, there were no visits—only phone calls. So the workers used this to their advantage. There were only two phones, and kids received ten minutes of talk time. Little did the kids know that Chris and JW had quite the surprise for them. Instead of talking to their mother or grandmother, they were welcomed with a "what you doing with yo lil bad tail."

129

Each kid that got on the phone had a magical smile appear on their face as soon as they heard Chris's or JW's voice. They told the kids to be cool and to do right. Even without being there, the two of them made an impact on these boys that could not be broken. Respect? Admiration? No, these boys loved them, and it was clear. The phone calls seemed to restore the balance for a while. Things were back to normal. The phone call was helpful for JW but did nothing but twist the dagger that was already present in Chris's heart. He felt guiltier by the second. He truly felt like he had abandoned the kids. He spent his nights worrying about them. *What have I done? These boys believed in me. I was so close to helping them.*

He thought about JC telling him that he was the closest thing he ever had to a father. He thought about the class and how the boys shared their heart with him. How they trusted him. And how he felt like he had betrayed them. Chris was beating himself up worse than any whupping that he had received from Clemmie D. *God, what did I do to deserve this curse? I know I wasn't following the rules, but was I wrong to be there for those kids? Didn't they need the love that I gave them? Oh, Jesus, what did I do? Why is this happening to me?*

Chris had always desired to hear from God directly, but he always seemed to receive his answers in a different form of communication. Some people have their dreams. Some people get prophecy. But Chris always received a sign, something that he couldn't deny if he wanted to.

Chris was walking around the mall with Lisa and he saw one of his kids from the detention center. It was Isaiah. His immediate reaction was to attempt to stay out of sight. Lisa saw that Chris appeared to be hiding. "Baby, what are you doing?"

Chris looked at her and said, "That's one of the kids from the detention center. We are not allowed to have any outside contact with anyone that has been in the facility."

Lisa looked at Chris like he was stupid. "Baby, what they gonna do, fire you? You don't work there anymore. Go over there and talk to that boy."

Chris had forgotten that he was no longer part of the detention center. He was free to talk to any of the kids, including the females. He walked over to Isaiah. Isaiah looked up at Chris and began to cry. He ran to him and hugged him. "Chris! Man, bro, what's up! I was just telling my mom about you. How are you doing?"

Chris was frozen. His mind was going a billion miles a minute. Finally he spoke. "I'm doing good, sir. I would ask you how you are doing, but I see you cheesin' like you trying out for a Kool-Aid commercial."

They shared laughter and the rest of the evening together. Lisa sat back and cried as she viewed the happiness of both Chris and the young man.

She closed her eyes and placed her hand on her chest. *Thank you, God. Thank you for this man. Thank you for his heart. Thank you, Jesus. Thank you.*

Chris had received his revelation. What he had viewed as the worst thing that could happen ended up being the best thing for him. He had not lost a job. He had lost limitation. The job was just a temporary mission for him. His mission was far past the walls of JDC. Instead of helping them when they came to JDC, he could help them before they ever got there. Chris began to get in contact of the families of the kids he had come across to see how they were doing. He began to get involved with their lives. It wasn't long before he received a text that said meet me at the Cage on Treadway, 8:00 p.m.

After JC got out, his first destination was to see Chris. When 8:00 p.m. rolled around, Chris pulled up to the court. Chris and JC greeted with a warm embrace. "What's up, Pops?"

Chris was elated. "How are you, son? I'm glad to see you out."

JC Laughed. "Well, you shouldn't be, Pops. 'Cause now I'm gonna have to give you that whuppin' I promised you on this here court."

Chris smiled but said no words. He walked to the top of the key and slammed the ball on the ground. JC happily accepted the challenge. As the two of them were playing, a couple of all-black Chevy Tahoes pulled up. It seemed that word travelled fast that JC was out, and Chris wasn't the only one ready to greet him. JC was dribbling at the top of the key and looked up and saw Cobra getting out the car. JC froze. Chris stole the ball and went in for a basket but saw that JC was staring off into the distance. He saw that the young man was clearly frightened by something.

Cobra walked up to JC. "Well, young blood, I see you survived. Ha. You a little tougher than I thought."

JC was temporarily suffering from paralysis. His muscles would not move. He could not even talk. He just knew that he was about to be shot.

"What's wrong, young blood? You act like you seen a ghost. You ain't got nothing to say?"

Chris had heard of Cobra but never had a face to put with the name. But Chris new Cobra all too well. He just didn't know him as Cobra. "Damon Wills!" Chris shouted.

Cobra turned around quickly to see what fool was dumb enough to call him by that name.

"What? Damon, you don't remember me? It's lil Chris. Clemmie D's lil boy."

Now it was Cobra that felt like he had just seen a ghost. Chris and Cobra were as thick as thieves growing up. As a matter of fact, Chris's grandpa was Cobra's father figure. Cobra's associates were lost.

"Damon Wills is dead. Don't call me that no more. I'm Cobra now. And you might want to leave, lil Chris. I got some unfinished business with Mr. Carter here. I'll give you a pass for old time's sake and act like you were never here."

Chris walked over and stood in front of JC. "Well, I'm sorry, Mr. Cobra. I'm not going to be able to do that. Whatever you doin' bro, you have to stop. What happened to you, bro?"

Cobra stood there silently boiling until he exploded. "I'm not your brother! Stop actin' like we back at the park! Stop acting like you know me! If you was my brother, you would have never let them take me. If you was my brother, you would have been there. Where was you at when they took me to that boys' home? Where was you at when my daddy beat my momma till she almost killed herself? Where was you when CPS took me from her 'cause she got on them drugs? Don't come to me tryin' to act brand-new. You had a family. You had everything I wanted. I loved your grandma and grandpa. Why didn't they just take me in? Why couldn't I have a daddy like you? Why? Why?"

Chris walked up to Cobra, but Cobra pulled out his 9mm and pointed at Chris and said, "No! You get the hell away from me. Don't you come near me!"

Chris began to speak. "No, you not gonna to put this on me, Damon. I looked everywhere for you. I asked everyone, and they told me that they didn't know where you were. My papa went to your mom's house and asked about you. She said that ya'll were moving away and that she had already sent you to live with your sister. My papa cried when he found out you was gone. I had only seen my papa cry twice in his life before he got cancer. And one of the reasons he cried was because of you. He begged your mom to let him know where ya'll were going to be staying. He was going to let both of ya'll move in with us. He sat me down and asked me how I felt about ya'll moving in and about me sharing a room with you. He even told me that we could get bunk beds. We didn't know, Cobra. All this time, we thought that ya'll left us!"

Cobra fell to his knees and began to cry. I'm not talking about a few tears and a sniffle. I mean that ugly cry—that cry that your aunty gives at a funeral when she's trying to jump into the casket with the person. Cobra looked up at Chris. "Did Mr. Daughtery really want me? Was he really gonna let me stay with ya'll?"

Chris fell to his knees and looked at Cobra eye to eye. "I promise, Damon. He loved you like you were his own. He asked about you all the time until he saw that it hurt me. So he stopped asking. Whether you were with us or not, you never stopped being his son."

Cobra began to cry even harder than before. He jumped to his feet, pushed Chris out of the way, and put the gun against JC's forehead. JC closed his eyes as his heart tried to beat out of his chest, and the tears streamed down his face. Chris shouted to him, "Damon, I'm begging you. For me. Please let this stuff with JC go. I'm sorry for what happened to you. It wasn't right, and I promise I know that. You were a good kid that got put in a bad situation."

Cobra shouted back at him, "Why should I give one single care about him. Nobody cared about me. Didn't no one come save me? Didn't no one say no don't do that to him? No, it wasn't him that shot that man. No, don't take him to prison. Who was there for me? Your *I'm sorry's* don't mean crap to me now. You will never know what I went through. But somebody is going to feel my pain. This lil bastard right here is going to understand. Open your eyes and look at me. Look at me, dangit!"

JC opened his eyes. He saw the pain and the rage in the man's eyes. Just as it seemed that Cobra was going to pull the trigger, Chris shouted, "What would Paw Paw say? What if he is looking at you right now? Could you pull the trigger in front of him? I understand now. No one was there for you. Maybe I failed you because we didn't go get you earlier, but dangit, Damon, I didn't know. I would have come for you. Paw Paw would have come for you. JC is just like you. No one was there for him. But I have the chance to give JC what you were looking for. Don't take that from him. Don't take that from me. Don't take that from Paw Paw because as long as we live, a piece of him is alive."

Cobra's arm began to tremble. He began to hear the things that Mr. Daughtery (Paw Paw) had told him. He remembered how he was always trying to help someone else. He remembered the ball games and pizza places and theme parks that he used to take them to. But more than anything, he remembered how it made him feel when he called him *son*. Cobra lowered his gun and continued to stare JC in the eyes. "I hope you know how lucky you are to have Chris. You best not ever forget. I'm letting this pass as a favor to him and Mr. Daughtery. But you owe me something in return."

JC was too frightened to answer, so he nodded his head and waited to hear what debt he would have to repay.

Cobra paused for a second and looked at all the people that surrounded him. "You have to promise that you will never turn out like me. All that player stuff and gangster stuff has to stop. Be the man that I could have been. You listen to him. It's not a day goes by that I don't wish I went a different way."

He attempted to walk away, but Chris ran to him. "Damon. It don't have to be like this. I didn't get a chance to stop you before, but I have my chance now. I'm not letting you go this time."

Cobra laughed. "It's too late for me, Chris. I've done too much. I've done my dirt, and I will pay for it."

Chris interrupted him. "My Papa—I mean our Papa—taught me that Saul was one of the most evil people in the Bible and God took the devils number one draft pick and made him into the most anointed preacher in the Bible, so don't tell me that God can't use you. It's your past that will give others hope."

JC walked up to Cobra. "You told me once that you was going to look out for me and that we were family. Well, family don't quit on each other. So how about you come to church with me and my mom on Sunday?"

Both Cobra and Chris were shocked. Cobra inquired as to JC's actions. "Man, I just pulled a gun on you. I was about to take your life. I had people whup yo tail in jail. And you telling me that we family and you want me to come to church with you? Why would you say this to me? I don't understand."

JC looked at Chris and smiled. "They did much worse than that to Jesus and he still died for us. That's what happens when you let Jesus in your life."

Chris felt far past convicted. All he could think about was Holley. Cobra looked at JC as he had his hand stretched out for a handshake. "Well, young blood, if you can forgive me for all that, then the least I can do is go to church. What time is service?"

They all shook hands. JC walked over to Chris. "Thank you. I owe you my life."

Chris laughed. "No, you owe Jesus your life. You owe me this game we bout to finish."

Julian chuckled. "Ha, I'm in a good mood. I won't even dunk on you no more!"

JC had closed one door of his past, but one still stood wide open. He texted Cherish and told her to meet him at the school gym. JC was shooting around as Cherish walked in and silently sat on the bleachers. She thought that JC had not noticed her presence. As JC was shooting a shot, he stopped and shouted, "Hey, this one is for you, Cherish."

After he swished the shot, he walked over to Cherish and sat on the seat below her. It was hard for Cherish to even look at him. She was fighting an emotional battle inside herself. She was so angry with what JC had done. Part of her wanted to scream obscenities at the top of her lungs while the other side wanted to run into JC's arms and be held by the boy that had inadvertently stolen her heart. Her heart was in a tug of war.

JC noticed her inner disturbance. "I'm sorry does not do justice for the damage I may have caused you. I was just so . . . I wanted to be . . . it wasn't like you think it was but . . . well, it was like that after you did that, but . . ." JC had no grasp on what he was trying to say. He stumbled and talked in broken sentences. This is the first time he had ever cared how things came out. This was a completely new side of JC. Before his life-changing experiences, he would have fluently spit out an emotionless explanation for his actions without ever pausing to take a breath. But things were different now. He was different now.

He took a second to try and get his thoughts together. "Look, Cherish, when you told me no all those times, it intrigued me. The challenge seemed fun. But once we spent time that night, I felt something that I had never felt before. That night you had more than my interest. You had my heart. My first intentions were to knock you down, but that all changed after we left the movies. Honestly, you are the first girl I ever really talked to. You were so smart and different. But when you asked me what I was gonna do for you if we got together, all I could remember was what one of my coaches had told me. He said that all these h—girls—was just gonna try and get my money. So I thought that you was just trying to use me. So I used you before you could do it to me."

Cherish became angered. "JC, why would you think that? I was just asking you what you would do to make me feel special. My daddy always taught me that a man would love me and take care of me. I wasn't looking for money. I was looking for someone to care about me. When you told me you love me, it seemed so real. I had liked you for a long time, but I didn't like the way you were. You was always treating girls like dirt. Everyone told me that you was a dog, but that isn't what I saw in you. I saw a good person that didn't know he was a good person. I saw that guy you showed me at the park that night. I'm not gonna lie, JC. I want to hate you. I want you to know my pain. But as much as I want that, I just want to be there for you. I want to know that you are all right, and that just pisses me off even more. You hurt me so bad with what you did. I don't think you will ever know."

Cherish tried to turn away from JC, but he jumped up to get face-to-face with her. He looked her in her eyes and began to let his heart speak. "I think I do. I can't tell you how many nights I spent at JDC thinkin' about what I would say to you. I heard you over and over again in my head. I heard you tell me that no one would ever love me."

Cherish's lips began to quiver, and she was submerged in a sea of guilt. She remembered that day. "JC, I didn't mean that. I just said it because I was—"

JC interrupted her. "No, let me finish. I thought that you were right. I thought that I would never know what love was. But I met this guy named Chris, and he introduced me to God. I prayed for this day so many times, and now it's here. I begged God for the chance to make it right. To right the wrongs that I had done to you. So I'm gonna take this chance I'm given."

He grabbed Cherish's hands and looked into her eyes. Cherish had not a clue what to think. She was neither positive nor negative in her thinking. She was neutral. This was more dangerous for her because it left her in the most vulnerable position. JC began to cry and sweat at the same time. They stood there in a silent stare for a few minutes.

Finally JC spoke, "Close your eyes and bow your head." Cherish was confused but obeyed. "Dear God, thank you for this chance. Thank you for your forgiveness that you have given me. Now I pray that you give Cherish the freedom to forgive me and give me the strength to forgive myself. God, you have shown me so much in such a short time, and I'm so thankful for you. In that prayer in Matthews, Jesus, you said, forgive us our debts as we forgive our debtors. So now that's what I'm praying for. Not only forgiveness but healing from the pain that we have caused each other. I love her, God. Thank you. Amen."

Cherish fell to her knees in a tsunami of tears. JC was confused. He dropped to his knees in concern and asked, "What's wrong, Cherish?"

She looked up and spoke through her tears, "JC, I love you too. I have never had a guy pray for me. And I forgive you, JC. I forgive you." Cherish lunged into JC's arms and began to kiss him.

JC began to think to himself, *OH . . . MY . . . GOD! This feels so good.* This was far past the emotionless sexual acts that he had become accustomed to. This kiss put butterflies in his stomach. His heart began to flutter. He could not move any part of his body. This was something serious. After the kiss, JC was intoxicated by the passion that he had just experienced for the first time.

Cherish smiled. "Well, judging by your face, that was as good to you as it was to me. So now that you know what I mean when I asked you, what are you gonna do for me if we get together?"

JC's first thought was "Girl, I will do whatever you want for feelings like that!" But his thoughts were short-lived. "Cherish, I can't."

She had a drastic change in tone. "What do you mean you can't? Are you telling me that you don't want to be with me? JC, I don't care what happened in the past. I told you I forgive you. I want to be with you. You've changed now. You are being that good person that I know you can be."

JC shook his head. "No, it's not like that. I do want to be with you. I want that so bad. I want to be your man. I want to treat you right. But before I do that, I have to get right. I have not truly been tested yet, Cherish. I love you and care about you too much to make a decision like this off of emotion. I need to get closer to God. I need to be the man you deserve before I even approach you that way. It is not worth the risk. I refuse to hurt you again. Please don't be mad at me, but can we just be friends?"

Cherish was completely blown away by what JC had just done. His words did nothing but make her desire him even more. "I understand, and I would love to be your friend—under one condition."

JC didn't do too well with conditions, so he made no promises and waited for her to state her stipulation. "You have to teach me more about God. I'm very interested in getting to know him."

JC smiled as placed his head against hers as they sat in the empty gym.

It did not take long for Holley to get fired behind all that had happened. She began to drink even more heavily than before. She lost all hope for her life. She just needed one thing to push her over the edge. She looked at her phone and saw that she had a call from a number that looked familiar but she didn't know. She picked up the phone and said hello.

"Is this Holley?"

She instantly knew who it was. She began to get upset because she thought that he was calling to taunt her about losing her job. "Look, you bastard, don't call me so you can make fun of me about losing my job. That's why I got you fired—'cause you think you are so great. Well, yeah, I got fired, but you lost your job first. How do you like that? I got you before you could get me."

There was a slight pause. Her statements did get to Chris a little bit, but he remembered what he heard JC say. "They did much worse to Jesus, and he still died for us." Chris took a deep breath and began to speak. "Look, Holley, I'm not happy about you getting fired. I was calling to see if you were okay."

Holley was not buying it. "Don't try that bull with me. I know you hate me. I know that you are happy to see me in pain. You don't even know what I'm going through—"

Chris cut her off. "Look, I'm not going to lie, Holley. You been doing shady stuff to me ever since I called you out for trying to talk to me. I lost respect for you after that. Yes, I was pissed with all you did to JC and JW.

It just wasn't right. But I never stopped to think what you must be going through to do this much to someone else."

Holley's anger came to a screeching halt. That was the last thing she expected to hear, but it opened her ears.

"Look, I want to tell you sorry for how I ignored you and never gave you the compassion or patience that you deserved. I never tried to understand you or your situation. So I would love to meet up for lunch and give you the chance to speak on some of the things that you are going through."

Holley just began to cry and ask why. She could not understand what Chris was doing, but she knew she needed someone. She accepted his invite and met him at a restaurant. Holley wasted no time sharing her life story. Chris simply sat there and listened. She started with how her father used to rape her and her sisters and her mom. He continued to rape them even as adults. Her father was actually the father of her first 2 kids. She talked about how many foster homes she had been in. She said that one foster family just packed up and moved one day. They completely forgot about her because she was so quiet. They came back to get one last box, and she was sitting on the back porch because the house was locked when she got home. They just took her back to the orphanage and never told her good-bye. They simply told the manager that they shouldn't keep her.

This all made sense to Chris. This is why she needed attention so bad and why she took whatever she could get. Chris handed Holley some napkins for her face.

She continued by telling him how her husband was a good man but never had time for her because he was always at work. She felt terrible for cheating on him, but she needed something from a man. She talked about how the kids always asked for him and never seemed to want her. Chris knew that she needed help, so he called for reinforcements.

"Holley, this is Tomika. She has an amazing gift of ministry. I feel like she will be healthy for you."

Holley did not want to look at Tomika after all the trouble she had caused, but Tomika calmed her fears. "How are you doing, Mrs. Holley? Look, I know that you may think I have it out for you, but I promise you that I have no ill will towards you. I'm going to tell you something that a friend once told me. I'm going to teach you what love is."

This statement scared her to her very core. "Why would you do that after all I did to you?"

"Because I remember where I was before someone showed me what love was."

Holley began to cry, and Tomika just held her. "It's okay, baby. Jesus is going to fix this."

Erin went back to school to get her degree in psychology. She became a counselor under the church's Christian counseling service.

Julian started off working with some old friends but ended up finding his way to God and became a youth minister alongside Chris.

Holley had a rough road but also found her way to God and became a motivational speaker. She and Tomika traveled across America, giving their testimony and giving hope to all that heard it.

A lot of the kids from the detention center took the From Boys to Gentlemen class to heart. They even started to share some of the knowledge they learned with their friends and loved ones. Mouse went to college in Georgia and started his own version of the class. He called it Quit Trippin and Grow Up. I don't know about the name, but the class was good.

Tomika is simply blessed. She is still doing the motivational speaking and ministering at the church. She and JC had become closer than they had ever dreamed. She attributed everything to God. She had found love in not just one but two men. This was something that she had longed for all her life. Between Jesus and JC, she forgot all about the possibility of having a husband. But God has a funny way of reminding you.

JC had made a 180. He had given a public apology to all the schools and even went as far as to give the local news an interview about his time spent in the detention center. Now don't think for a second that his popularity with the ladies had done anything but increased with his recent visit to jail. But JC was focused on other things. He became a community-service star. He held basketball camps and visited youth centers all over the state.

At one of the youth centers in town, a young boy walked up to JC and began to show his admiration. "Wow, you are Julian Carter. Hey, man, I want to be just like you when I grow up. My brother says that you be getting all the girls and don't even have to try. He said that you such a player that your teachers be trying to get at you. That is so tight. You pullin' hoes like Wayne. I bet you are going to pull all the hoes when you go to college, huh?"

JC looked at the young man and said very calmly yet sternly, "No."

The young man was puzzled. "No? Why not, bro? You know they are going to be throwing they self at you."

JC smiled and put his arm around the young man and said, "Because I don't want nobody to do that to my mama or my future daughter. Hey, let me tell you a little story . . ."

This book is a collaboration of true stories mixed with some fiction.

Edwards Brothers Malloy
Oxnard, CA USA
March 30, 2016